Pumpkin Spice and Everything Nice

Gracelynne MacAllister

Published by Trilogy Ink, 2024.

Chapter 1: The First Taste of Autumn

The air in Willow Creek had that crisp, golden quality that signaled the beginning of autumn. Leaves were just beginning to turn, their edges kissed by the first hints of orange and red. Emma Harper, standing behind the counter of her bakery, took a deep breath, savoring the scent of cinnamon and nutmeg that filled the room. It was the first day of October, and she was ready to unveil her latest creation: Pumpkin Spice Scones with a Maple Glaze.

The bell above the door jingled, and Emma looked up with a smile, her hazel eyes brightening at the sight of Mrs. Thompson, one of her regulars. The elderly woman made her way to the counter, leaning on her cane as she gazed around the cozy interior of *Harper's Bakery*.

"Morning, Mrs. Thompson," Emma greeted, her Scottish accent softened by years in the States but still unmistakable. "I've got something new for you today."

Mrs. Thompson's eyes twinkled with curiosity. "You always know how to tempt an old lady, Emma. What do you have for me?"

Emma reached behind the counter and presented a scone, its golden surface drizzled with a thick, glossy glaze. "Pumpkin Spice Scones with Maple Glaze. Just in time for the festival."

The older woman took a careful bite, her eyes closing as she savored the flavor. "Oh, my dear, this is heavenly. You've outdone yourself."

Emma blushed slightly, always a little shy when it came to compliments. "I'm glad you like it. I was up half the night perfecting the recipe."

As Mrs. Thompson continued to enjoy her scone, the doorbell chimed again. This time, a man entered, his presence filling the small shop. He was tall, with broad shoulders and an easy smile that immediately caught Emma's attention. She couldn't recall seeing him in town before, and in a place like Willow Creek, new faces were rare.

"Good morning," the man said, his voice warm and rich. "I've heard great things about this bakery and thought I'd stop by."

Emma wiped her hands on her apron, feeling suddenly self-conscious. "Welcome to *Harper's Bakery*. What can I get for you?"

The man glanced at the display case, his eyes lingering on the scones. "I'll take one of those, please. And a cup of coffee, black."

As Emma prepared his order, she couldn't help but sneak glances at him. There was something about the way he carried himself—confident but not arrogant—that intrigued her. She handed him the scone and coffee, their hands brushing briefly.

"Are you new to town?" she asked, trying to sound casual.

He nodded, taking a sip of his coffee. "Just visiting, actually. I'm Ben Foster, a travel writer. I'm here to cover the pumpkin festival for a magazine."

Emma's heart skipped a beat. A writer in Willow Creek? That was certainly new. "I'm Emma Harper. This bakery has been in my family for generations."

"Nice to meet you, Emma," Ben said, smiling again. "This scone is incredible. You've got some serious talent."

Emma felt her cheeks warm again. "Thank you, Ben. I'm glad you like it."

They chatted for a few more minutes, exchanging pleasantries about the town and the upcoming festival. But all too soon, Ben finished his scone and drained the last of his coffee.

"I'll be back," he said as he stood to leave. "I'm looking forward to trying more of your creations, Emma."

As he walked out the door, Emma found herself smiling, a fluttery feeling in her chest that she hadn't felt in a long time. She watched him through the window as he walked down the street, wondering if his visit would be a brief one or if he might just stick around long enough for her to get to know him better.

The day continued with a steady stream of customers, but Emma's thoughts kept drifting back to Ben Foster, the travel writer with the easy smile. She had a feeling that this autumn in Willow Creek was going to be different from any other.

And as the leaves continued to turn and the days grew shorter, Emma knew one thing for certain: the season had only just begun, and there was so much more to come.

Chapter 2: A Town Full of Traditions

The next morning, Emma woke up to the familiar scent of coffee brewing in her small kitchen. She stretched, savoring the moment before the day's work began. As she pulled on a cozy sweater and tied her hair back, she couldn't help but think about Ben Foster. It wasn't every day that someone new came to Willow Creek, let alone someone as interesting as a travel writer.

Her mind was still on Ben as she walked to the bakery, the early morning mist giving the town an ethereal glow. She passed the town square, where preparations for the annual Pumpkin Festival were well underway. Booths were being set up, and the large field behind the town hall was already filled with bright orange pumpkins, just waiting for the contest to begin.

Emma loved this time of year. The festival was one of Willow Creek's most cherished traditions, a celebration that brought everyone together. From pumpkin carving contests to the grand costume ball, it was a time for the community to revel in the spirit of Halloween. And for Emma, it was a chance to showcase her baking skills to the entire town—and now, it seemed, to a travel writer as well.

As she approached the bakery, she noticed a familiar face waiting by the door. It was Mabel, the town's unofficial gossip, who seemed to have a sixth sense for sniffing out new information.

"Good morning, Emma!" Mabel called out, her eyes twinkling with mischief. "I heard there was a new man in town, and that he visited your bakery yesterday."

Emma unlocked the door and pushed it open, holding it for Mabel as she followed her inside. "Good morning, Mabel. Yes, his name is Ben Foster. He's a travel writer, here to cover the festival."

Mabel's eyebrows shot up. "A writer, you say? Well, isn't that something! You'll have to keep an eye on him, Emma. Who knows what kind of stories he'll find in our little town."

Emma smiled as she set about preparing the bakery for the day. "I'm sure he'll find plenty to write about. Willow Creek is full of surprises, after all."

As the morning rush began, Emma found herself slipping into the comforting routine of kneading dough, rolling out pastry, and serving her customers with a smile. But every now and then, her thoughts would return to Ben, wondering what he was up to and if he really would come back to the bakery.

Her question was answered just after lunch when the bell above the door chimed, and there he was, looking every bit as charming as the day before. Emma's heart gave a small leap, and she wiped her hands on her apron before stepping out from behind the counter.

"Back for more, I see," she said, her voice light.

Ben grinned, his eyes crinkling at the corners. "I couldn't resist. Those scones were too good not to have again."

"Well, I'm glad to hear it. Can I get you something different this time? Maybe a slice of pumpkin pie?"

Ben nodded. "That sounds perfect."

As Emma prepared his order, Ben leaned against the counter, watching her with an appreciative smile. "You know, this town really is something special. Everywhere I go, people seem to know each other, and there's a warmth here that you don't find in a lot of places."

Emma handed him the plate with a slice of pie, the crust golden and flaky, the filling a deep, rich orange. "That's Willow Creek for you. We're a close-knit community, especially around this time of year. The festival is one of our oldest traditions."

Ben took a bite of the pie, his expression turning thoughtful. "It's exactly what I've been looking for. Something real, something with heart. I think I'm going to enjoy writing about this place."

Emma felt a swell of pride for her town. "I hope you do. There's so much history here, so many stories waiting to be told."

Ben nodded, taking another bite. "I'd love to hear some of them, if you're willing to share."

Emma hesitated for a moment, then smiled. "I'd be happy to. Maybe I could show you around, introduce you to some of the folks who've lived here all their lives. They have more stories than I could ever tell."

Ben's smile widened. "I'd like that, Emma. I'd like that a lot."

As the afternoon wore on, Emma found herself talking to Ben about the town, the festival, and her family's bakery. The conversation flowed easily, and before she knew it, the sun was beginning to set, casting a golden hue over the town.

As Ben stood to leave, he paused by the door. "Thank you for today, Emma. I'll take you up on that offer to show me around. How about tomorrow?"

Emma nodded, a warm feeling spreading through her chest. "Tomorrow sounds perfect. I'll see you then."

As she locked up the bakery that evening, Emma couldn't help but smile. She hadn't felt this excited in a long time, and she was looking forward to what the next day would bring.

Chapter 3: The Tour of Willow Creek

The next day dawned with the promise of clear skies and cool breezes, perfect weather for a tour of Willow Creek. Emma arrived at the bakery early, as usual, preparing fresh batches of pastries and bread for the morning rush. Her thoughts kept drifting to her planned tour with Ben, a nervous excitement bubbling up whenever she pictured his easy smile and the way he seemed genuinely interested in the town.

By mid-morning, the bakery was bustling with regulars, but Emma couldn't help glancing at the door every time the bell jingled. When Ben finally walked in, right on time, Emma felt a mix of relief and excitement. He was dressed casually in jeans and a flannel shirt, looking every bit the part of someone blending into small-town life.

"Good morning, Emma," Ben greeted her with a warm smile. "Ready to show me the secrets of Willow Creek?"

"Morning, Ben. I'm all set." Emma wiped her hands on her apron and untied it, hanging it on a hook behind the counter. "Let's start with the town square. It's the heart of our Halloween festivities."

They stepped out into the crisp autumn air, the town already abuzz with activity as vendors set up their stalls for the festival. The town square was a picturesque spot, with its old-fashioned lampposts, benches, and the large fountain in the center. Orange and black bunting hung from every available surface, giving the place a festive atmosphere.

Emma pointed to the fountain. "This is where we have the pumpkin carving contest every year. People come from all over to compete. Some of the carvings are truly incredible."

Ben nodded, taking out a small notebook and jotting down some notes. "I can see why. This town has a certain charm, like it's straight out of a storybook."

They continued their tour, with Emma pointing out various landmarks, each with its own bit of history. The old church, where the bell tower was rumored to be haunted; the general store, which had been in business since the town was founded; and the small, cozy library that hosted ghost story readings every Halloween.

As they walked, the conversation flowed naturally, moving from the history of the town to more personal topics. Ben asked Emma about her bakery, and she found herself telling him stories about her grandmother, who had taught her everything she knew about baking.

"She always said that food brings people together," Emma reminisced. "And that's what I try to do with the bakery. It's not just about selling pastries; it's about creating a space where people can come together and feel at home."

Ben looked at her thoughtfully. "You've done a great job with that. I felt it the moment I walked in."

Emma smiled, touched by his words. "Thank you, Ben. That means a lot."

They reached the edge of town, where the woods began. Emma hesitated, then pointed to a path that wound through the trees. "This is the trail to Hollow's Point. It's where we have the haunted hayride. They say the woods are enchanted, especially around Halloween."

Ben raised an eyebrow. "Enchanted? How so?"

Emma grinned, feeling a bit mischievous. "There are stories about people seeing strange lights in the trees, hearing voices in the wind, and even encountering spirits. It's all part of the Halloween fun, of course."

"Of course," Ben said with a smile, but there was a hint of curiosity in his eyes.

They continued walking, the conversation turning to more lighthearted topics. Emma found herself laughing more than she had in a long time, enjoying Ben's company and the easy way he made her feel comfortable. The day passed quickly, and by the time they returned to the town square, the sun was beginning to set, casting long shadows across the ground.

"Thank you for the tour, Emma," Ben said as they reached the bakery. "I feel like I've really gotten to know this place. And I've got plenty to write about."

"I'm glad you enjoyed it," Emma replied, feeling a little sad that the day was ending. "You know where to find me if you have any more questions."

Ben paused, as if considering something, then smiled. "Actually, I was wondering if you'd like to join me for dinner tonight. There's a little place just outside of town I've heard good things about."

Emma's heart skipped a beat. "Dinner? That sounds... nice. I'd love to."

"Great," Ben said, his smile widening. "I'll pick you up at seven?"

"I'll be ready," Emma replied, her excitement growing.

As Ben walked away, Emma watched him go, a mix of anticipation and nervousness swirling inside her. This was more than just a friendly dinner; it felt like the beginning of something special. And for the first time in a long time, Emma felt a flutter of hope in her heart.

The sun dipped below the horizon, casting the town in a warm, golden glow. As Emma walked back into her bakery, she couldn't help but smile. This autumn was turning out to be even more magical than she had imagined.

Chapter 4: A Dinner to Remember

Emma stood in front of her closet, sifting through her clothes with a growing sense of frustration. Why was it so hard to find something to wear? It wasn't as if she didn't have nice clothes, but nothing seemed quite right for dinner with Ben. She wanted to look good, but not like she was trying too hard.

Finally, she settled on a simple but elegant dress in a deep shade of burgundy, paired with a light cardigan to ward off the evening chill. She let her hair fall in loose waves around her shoulders and added a touch of makeup, just enough to bring out her eyes. Taking one last look in the mirror, she took a deep breath and nodded to herself. This would do.

At exactly seven, the doorbell rang. Emma felt her heart skip a beat as she walked to the door, her nerves suddenly flaring up. But when she opened it and saw Ben standing there with that easy smile of his, she felt a wave of calm wash over her.

"Wow, you look amazing," Ben said, his eyes warm with appreciation.

Emma blushed, feeling a bit shy. "Thank you, Ben. You clean up pretty well yourself."

Ben chuckled, offering her his arm. "Shall we?"

They walked to Ben's car, and as they drove out of town, the conversation flowed easily between them. The restaurant Ben had chosen was a quaint little place nestled on the outskirts of

Willow Creek, with fairy lights twinkling in the trees and a soft glow emanating from the windows.

Inside, the atmosphere was cozy and intimate, with candlelit tables and soft music playing in the background. They were seated by a window that offered a view of the surrounding woods, the trees swaying gently in the evening breeze.

As they perused the menu, Emma found herself relaxing, the earlier nervousness melting away. Ben was easy to talk to, and she was quickly realizing how much they had in common. They both loved small towns, cherished traditions, and shared a deep appreciation for the simpler things in life.

Over dinner, they talked about their lives, their dreams, and the paths that had led them to Willow Creek. Emma found herself opening up to Ben in a way she hadn't with anyone in a long time. She told him about her grandmother's bakery, how it had been a place of comfort and refuge for her after her parents had passed away. Ben listened attentively, his expression thoughtful as he absorbed every word.

"And what about you?" Emma asked, curious to learn more about him. "How did you become a travel writer?"

Ben smiled, taking a sip of his wine. "I've always loved to travel, even as a kid. I guess you could say I've been chasing stories my whole life. Writing about the places I visit just felt like a natural extension of that. But lately..." He paused, his gaze distant. "Lately, I've been feeling like I'm missing something. Like there's more to life than just wandering from one place to the next."

Emma nodded, understanding the sentiment. "It must be hard, not having a place to call home."

"It is," Ben admitted. "But coming here, to Willow Creek, has been different. There's something about this town that feels... right. Like I could actually put down roots here."

Emma's heart fluttered at his words, a small hope blossoming in her chest. "Maybe you've finally found what you're looking for."

"Maybe," Ben said, his eyes locking with hers. "Or maybe I just found the person who makes me want to stay."

The intensity in his gaze made Emma's breath catch in her throat. She wasn't sure how to respond, but before she could say anything, their waiter arrived with dessert—a decadent pumpkin cheesecake that looked too good to resist.

The moment passed, but the atmosphere between them remained charged with unspoken possibilities. They shared the dessert, savoring each bite, and by the time they finished, Emma felt like she was floating on air.

As they left the restaurant and drove back to town, the conversation was lighter, filled with laughter and teasing. But underneath it all, there was a growing connection, a sense that something special was beginning to take shape between them.

When they reached Emma's bakery, Ben walked her to the door, the night air cool and crisp around them. Emma hesitated, feeling a mix of anticipation and uncertainty. She wasn't sure what to expect, but Ben seemed to sense her hesitation.

"Thank you for tonight, Emma," he said softly. "I had a great time."

"Me too," Emma replied, her voice barely above a whisper.

Ben smiled, a slow, warm smile that sent a shiver down her spine. He reached out and gently tucked a strand of hair behind her ear, his touch light and reassuring. "Good night, Emma."

"Good night, Ben," Emma whispered, her heart pounding in her chest.

As he walked away, Emma watched him go, her emotions swirling in a confusing mix of excitement, hope, and a little bit of fear. This was new, unexpected, and she wasn't sure where it was going. But for the first time in a long time, she was willing to find out.

She closed the door behind her, leaning against it for a moment as she tried to calm her racing heart. This autumn was indeed turning out to be something special, and Emma couldn't wait to see what the next day would bring.

Chapter 5: The Afterglow

The next morning, Emma found herself moving through the motions of her routine with a lighter heart. There was a new energy in the air, and she couldn't help but feel that it had everything to do with the dinner she had shared with Ben the night before. His words, the way he looked at her, and the warmth of his touch still lingered in her mind.

As she unlocked the bakery and stepped inside, the familiar scent of dough and spices greeted her. She set to work, kneading dough for the day's first batch of bread, but her thoughts kept drifting back to the way Ben had made her feel. It was as if a door had been opened to something new, something she hadn't even realized she was missing.

The bell above the door chimed, and Emma looked up, expecting to see one of her regulars. But to her surprise, it was Ben, standing in the doorway with a smile that seemed to light up the room.

"Good morning," he greeted, his voice warm and cheerful.

"Morning, Ben," Emma replied, her heart skipping a beat. "You're up early."

"I couldn't resist coming by," Ben said, walking over to the counter. "After last night, I wanted to see you again."

Emma felt her cheeks flush with warmth. "I'm glad you did."

Ben glanced around the bakery, taking in the scent of freshly baked goods. "Anything special on the menu today?"

"I'm trying out a new recipe," Emma said, pulling out a tray of warm cinnamon rolls from the oven. "Cinnamon rolls with a hint of pumpkin spice. Want to be my taste tester?"

"Absolutely," Ben replied, his eyes lighting up.

Emma plated a roll for him, and he took a bite, his expression one of pure contentment. "Emma, this is incredible. You've got a real gift."

"Thank you," Emma said, smiling. "It's always a bit nerve-wracking trying something new."

"Well, I'd say this one's a hit," Ben said, finishing the roll. "You've got a knack for knowing what people will love."

They talked for a while longer, their conversation flowing easily as they discussed the upcoming festival and the various events Ben planned to cover for his article. Emma felt more at ease with him than she had with anyone in a long time, and she couldn't help but marvel at how quickly he had become a part of her life.

As the morning rush began, Ben stood to leave, but not before promising to return later in the day. "I'm looking forward to that tour of the festival you promised," he said with a grin.

"Me too," Emma replied, watching him go.

The rest of the day passed in a blur of activity. The bakery was busier than usual, with customers excited about the festival and eager to try Emma's new pumpkin spice creations. But no matter how hectic things got, Emma couldn't stop thinking about Ben and the way he had effortlessly slipped into her world.

As the afternoon wore on, Emma began to close up the bakery, her thoughts already turning to the evening ahead. She had agreed to meet Ben at the town square, where the festival was in full swing, and she was looking forward to showing him more of what made Willow Creek so special.

When she arrived at the square, the air was filled with the sounds of laughter, music, and the scent of roasted chestnuts and caramel apples. The festival was a celebration of all things autumn, with booths selling handmade crafts, local produce, and, of course, plenty of pumpkins.

Emma spotted Ben near the fountain, his face lit up with excitement as he took in the scene. When he saw her, his smile widened, and he made his way over to her, his eyes sparkling with enthusiasm.

"This place is amazing," Ben said, his voice full of awe. "I've covered a lot of festivals, but there's something truly special about this one."

"It's the heart of Willow Creek," Emma said, her own pride evident in her voice. "Everyone comes together to make it happen, and it's been a tradition for as long as I can remember."

Ben looked around, his gaze lingering on the families, couples, and friends enjoying the festivities. "You can feel the sense of community here. It's like everyone is connected in some way."

Emma nodded, her heart swelling with affection for her town. "That's what I love about this place. It's more than just a town—it's a family."

They spent the evening wandering through the festival, stopping at various booths to sample the treats and admire the crafts. Emma introduced Ben to many of the town's residents, each one eager to share their stories and traditions. Ben took notes, but more often than not, he was simply content to listen and absorb the atmosphere.

As the night wore on, they found themselves back at the fountain, the moon casting a soft glow over the square. The crowd had thinned out, leaving the two of them in a moment of quiet amidst the bustle.

"I'm glad you brought me here," Ben said, his voice soft. "This has been one of the best days I've had in a long time."

"Me too," Emma replied, feeling a warmth spread through her. "I'm glad you're here, Ben."

He looked at her then, his expression serious yet tender. "Emma, I know we haven't known each other for long, but I feel like there's something special between us. I don't want to rush things, but I also don't want to ignore what I'm feeling."

Emma's heart pounded in her chest, the sincerity in his words stirring something deep within her. "I feel it too, Ben," she admitted, her voice barely above a whisper.

Ben reached out, gently taking her hand in his. "I don't know what the future holds, but I want to see where this goes. If you're willing to take that chance with me."

Emma looked up at him, her heart swelling with hope and a touch of fear. But as she gazed into his eyes, she knew that this was a chance worth taking. "I'm willing, Ben."

A slow smile spread across Ben's face, and he squeezed her hand gently. "Then let's see where this takes us, together."

They stood there for a moment, the world around them fading away as they took the first step toward something new, something that felt like it had the potential to be truly special.

And as the festival lights twinkled around them, Emma couldn't help but feel that this autumn was the beginning of something wonderful—something she had never expected, but now couldn't imagine her life without.

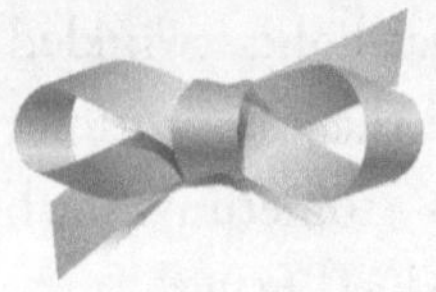

Chapter 6: Unfolding Possibilities

The next morning, Emma awoke with a sense of anticipation. Last night had felt like a turning point, a moment where possibilities began to take shape. She couldn't stop thinking about Ben, the way his hand had felt in hers, the sincerity in his voice when he'd said he wanted to see where things could go between them.

As she went about her morning routine, preparing the bakery for another busy day, Emma found herself smiling more than usual. The air was crisp and cool, the smell of autumn lingering in the breeze, and the excitement of the festival still buzzed throughout Willow Creek. But more than that, it was the memory of Ben that warmed her from within.

The morning rush at the bakery was steady, with regulars and festival-goers stopping in for their favorite treats. As she served customers and chatted with familiar faces, Emma's thoughts kept drifting to the evening ahead. She and Ben hadn't made specific plans, but she had a feeling he'd find a way to see her again today.

Sure enough, just before noon, the bell above the door jingled, and there was Ben, looking as effortlessly charming as ever. Emma's heart gave a little flutter as he walked over to the counter.

"Hey, Emma," Ben greeted her with a smile that made her feel like she was the only person in the room. "How's your day going?"

"Busy but good," Emma replied, returning his smile. "How about you? Getting a lot of material for your article?"

"More than I expected," Ben said, leaning against the counter. "But I have to admit, it's not just the festival that's been on my mind."

Emma's cheeks warmed, and she looked down at the tray of freshly baked cookies she was arranging. "I know what you mean."

Ben chuckled softly, and when Emma looked up, she saw that his gaze was warm, filled with that same mix of sincerity and affection she had seen the night before. "I was thinking," he began, "since you've shown me so much of the town, maybe I could take you somewhere special today. There's this place I've heard about just outside of Willow Creek, a little spot by the river. Thought it might be nice to get away from the festival crowd for a bit."

"That sounds perfect," Emma said, the idea of spending some quiet time with Ben away from the hustle and bustle appealing to her.

"Great," Ben said, his smile widening. "I'll pick you up around three?"

"Three it is," Emma agreed, feeling a flutter of excitement at the thought of their afternoon together.

The rest of the day passed in a blur of activity, with Emma counting down the hours until three. She kept busy with the bakery, but her thoughts were always on Ben and the possibilities that seemed to unfold every time they were together.

When the time finally came, Emma closed up the bakery and hurried home to change into something more suitable for an afternoon by the river. She chose a simple, comfortable outfit—jeans, a cozy sweater, and her favorite boots—something that would keep her warm but still look nice.

At exactly three, Ben arrived, and Emma couldn't help but feel a thrill of excitement as she climbed into his car. The drive out of town was peaceful, the scenery shifting from the familiar streets of Willow Creek to the more open, wooded areas surrounding it. They chatted easily, the conversation flowing naturally as they talked about their favorite outdoor spots and shared stories from their pasts.

When they arrived at the river, Emma was struck by how beautiful the place was. The water sparkled in the afternoon sunlight, and the trees lining the banks were a riot of autumn colors. A blanket of fallen leaves covered the ground, crunching softly underfoot as they walked along the river's edge.

"This place is amazing," Emma said, breathing in the fresh, crisp air. "How did you find out about it?"

"A local mentioned it to me when I was asking about good spots for photos," Ben explained, pulling a small camera out of his bag. "I thought it would be a great place to take some shots—and to relax."

Emma smiled, watching as Ben began to snap pictures of the scenery. There was something so peaceful about being out here with him, away from the noise and excitement of the festival. It felt like they were in their own little world, a place where they could just be themselves.

After a while, they found a spot to sit by the river, and Ben spread out a blanket he had brought with him. They sat down, the sound of the flowing water providing a soothing background to their conversation.

"So," Ben said, turning to her, "tell me more about you, Emma. What do you do when you're not running the best bakery in town?"

Emma laughed softly. "Well, the bakery takes up most of my time, but I love being outdoors, especially in the fall. There's something about the changing seasons that makes me feel alive. I also like to read, mostly cozy mysteries and romance novels—guess that makes me a bit of a cliché."

"Not at all," Ben said with a grin. "Sounds like you've got good taste. What about your family? You mentioned your grandmother taught you to bake."

Emma nodded, a fond smile on her lips. "She did. My grandmother was an incredible woman, and the bakery was her pride and joy. She passed away a few years ago, but I like to think she's still with me, especially when I'm baking. As for the rest of my family, it's just me now. My parents passed away when I was in my twenties, so it's been a while, but I've found a lot of support in the community here."

Ben's expression softened, and he reached out to take her hand, giving it a gentle squeeze. "I'm sorry, Emma. That must have been tough."

"It was," Emma admitted, feeling a lump in her throat. "But this town has always been my home, and the people here are like family. I guess that's why I've never felt the need to leave."

Ben nodded, understanding in his eyes. "I can see why you love it here. It's a special place. And I'm glad I came."

"Me too," Emma said, her voice soft.

They sat in comfortable silence for a while, just enjoying each other's company and the peaceful surroundings. As the sun began to dip lower in the sky, casting a warm golden light over the river, Emma felt a deep sense of contentment settle over her. She had never felt so at ease with someone, and the more time she spent with Ben, the more she realized how much she liked him—how much she wanted to see where this could go.

"Emma," Ben said after a while, his tone thoughtful, "I know this might seem sudden, but I've been thinking about what you said yesterday—about how this town feels like home. And I was wondering... if I decided to stick around a little longer, would that be okay with you?"

Emma's heart skipped a beat at his words, a surge of hope and excitement rising within her. "Ben, I would love it if you stayed."

Ben smiled, a look of relief and happiness on his face. "Then I guess I'm going to need to find a more permanent place to stay."

Emma laughed, the sound filled with joy. "I think that can be arranged. I happen to know a few people who might be able to help."

"Good," Ben said, his eyes locking with hers. "Because I'm not ready to leave this place—or you."

They sat there by the river, the sun setting behind them, casting the world in a soft, warm glow. And in that moment,

Emma knew that whatever the future held, she was ready to face it—because she wasn't facing it alone.

Chapter 7: A Sweet Decision

As the week progressed, the buzz of the Pumpkin Festival continued to fill the air in Willow Creek, but for Emma, everything seemed to revolve around Ben. Their time together at the river had only deepened the connection she felt with him, and she found herself eagerly anticipating every moment they could spend together.

The bakery had been busier than ever, with visitors coming in from out of town to enjoy the festival, but Emma didn't mind the hectic pace. In fact, it energized her, knowing that each day brought new opportunities to see Ben and explore what was growing between them.

One crisp morning, as Emma was rolling out dough for her signature pumpkin spice scones, she heard the familiar jingle of the bell above the door. She looked up, expecting to see one of her regulars, but instead, she found Ben standing in the doorway with a thoughtful expression.

"Morning, Emma," Ben greeted her, his smile a little more reserved than usual.

"Morning, Ben," Emma replied, wiping her hands on her apron as she walked over to him. "You look like you've got something on your mind."

Ben chuckled softly. "Is it that obvious?"

"Maybe just a little," Emma teased, though she couldn't shake the feeling that whatever was on his mind was serious. "What's up?"

Ben took a deep breath, his gaze steady as he met her eyes. "I've been thinking a lot about what we talked about at the river—about staying in Willow Creek longer. The thing is, I've always been on the move, never staying in one place for too long. But... I don't want to leave here. I don't want to leave you."

Emma's heart skipped a beat, her pulse quickening. "Ben, I don't want you to leave either."

"I've been talking to some of the locals," Ben continued, "and I think I might have found a way to make this work. There's an old house on the edge of town that's been empty for a while. It needs some work, but it's got potential. I was thinking... maybe I could fix it up, make it my home. That way, I could stay here for as long as I want."

Emma's heart swelled with emotion. The idea of Ben making Willow Creek his home—and making it their home—was more than she had dared to hope for. "Ben, that sounds... perfect. I'd love to help you fix it up if you'll let me."

Ben's eyes softened, and he reached out to take her hand, giving it a gentle squeeze. "I'd love that, Emma. I want us to build something together, something real."

Emma smiled, her heart full. "Then let's do it. Let's make Willow Creek your home."

Over the next few days, Emma and Ben worked together to start bringing the old house back to life. The place was charming in its own way, with a wraparound porch and large windows that let in plenty of light. It was clear that it had once been a beloved home, and as they cleaned and repaired, Emma could imagine the laughter and love that had once filled the rooms.

Working side by side, Emma and Ben grew even closer. They spent their days fixing up the house, and in the evenings, they would share meals, talk about their dreams, and plan for the future. It was as if the house was a symbol of their growing relationship—something that needed care, attention, and a little bit of hard work to flourish.

One evening, after a long day of painting and repairs, they sat on the porch, sipping hot cider and watching the stars come out. The air was cool, but the warmth of Ben's presence beside her made Emma feel like she was wrapped in a cozy blanket.

"You know," Ben said after a while, his voice thoughtful, "I've never felt this way about anyone before. It's like everything in my life has led me to this moment, to you."

Emma's heart fluttered at his words, and she looked over at him, her eyes shining. "I feel the same way, Ben. I never expected to meet someone like you, someone who just... fits into my life so perfectly."

Ben turned to her, his gaze intense and filled with emotion. "Emma, I don't want to rush things, but I want you to know that I'm serious about this—about us. I want to build a life with you here, in Willow Creek. I want to see where this can go."

Emma reached out, her hand resting on his cheek. "I want that too, Ben. More than anything."

Ben smiled, leaning in to press a gentle kiss to her lips. It was a kiss filled with promise, with the unspoken understanding that they were both ready to take the next step together.

As they sat there, wrapped in each other's arms, the future seemed brighter than ever. There would be challenges, of course—no journey worth taking was without its obstacles. But as long as they faced them together, Emma knew that they could make it through anything.

The old house was just the beginning, a foundation for the life they were starting to build. And as the autumn leaves fell around them, Emma couldn't help but feel that this was exactly where she was meant to be—right here, with Ben, in the place she loved most.

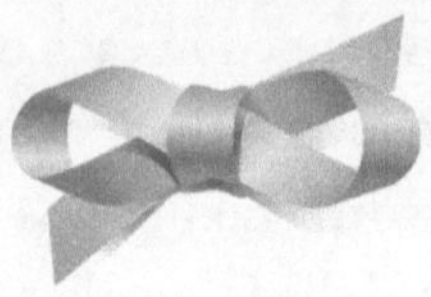

Chapter 8: A Twist of Fate

The following week brought a whirlwind of activity as Emma and Ben continued to work on the house. The days were long, but they were filled with laughter, shared meals, and a growing sense of companionship. It was as if they were building not just a home, but a life together, brick by brick and board by board.

As they painted the living room one afternoon, Emma paused, brush in hand, and looked at Ben. He was focused on the task at hand, but there was a relaxed ease in his movements, a contentment that mirrored her own. She couldn't help but smile, thinking of how far they had come in such a short time.

"Ben," Emma said, breaking the comfortable silence, "do you ever think about what brought you here? I mean, to Willow Creek?"

Ben looked up from his work, wiping a smudge of paint from his cheek. "All the time," he admitted. "It feels like everything in my life led me here, to this town, to you. It's strange, but in the best way."

Emma nodded, her thoughts turning inward. "I've lived here my whole life, and I've always loved it. But you... you've shown me a new side of Willow Creek. You've made me see it through your eyes, and it's made me love this place even more."

Ben walked over to her, taking the brush from her hand and setting it aside. "And you've made me see what it means to belong somewhere, Emma. I've never had that before, not really. But now... I feel like I've found my place, my person."

Emma's heart swelled with emotion, and she reached out to wrap her arms around him. "I'm so glad you came here, Ben. I can't imagine my life without you now."

Ben held her close, his voice soft. "You don't have to. I'm not going anywhere."

They stood there for a moment, wrapped in each other's embrace, the warmth of their connection filling the room. But just as Emma was about to pull back and return to their work, the sound of a car pulling into the driveway broke the silence.

Emma frowned, glancing out the window. "Are we expecting anyone?"

Ben shook his head. "Not that I know of."

Curious, they walked to the front door and stepped outside, where a sleek black car had just parked. The driver's door opened, and a tall man in a sharp suit stepped out. He looked out of place in the rustic surroundings, his presence commanding and a little intimidating.

"Ben Foster?" the man called out, his voice carrying across the yard.

Ben tensed beside Emma, his easygoing demeanor suddenly replaced with something more guarded. "That's me," he replied, stepping forward. "Who's asking?"

The man approached, his expression unreadable. "I'm Daniel Price, editor-in-chief of *Explore,* the magazine you've been freelancing for. We need to talk."

Emma felt a knot form in her stomach at the man's serious tone. She looked at Ben, who was clearly surprised—and not entirely pleased—by the unexpected visit.

"What's this about, Daniel?" Ben asked, his voice careful.

Daniel glanced at Emma, then back at Ben. "Can we talk privately?"

Ben hesitated, then nodded. "Sure. Let's go inside."

Emma watched as the two men disappeared into the house, her mind racing with questions. Who was this Daniel Price, and what did he want with Ben? She couldn't shake the feeling that whatever it was, it wasn't good news.

Inside, Ben led Daniel to the partially finished living room and gestured for him to sit. Daniel remained standing, his expression serious.

"Ben, I've been trying to reach you for days," Daniel began, his tone brisk. "I came here because I need an answer, and I need it now."

"An answer to what?" Ben asked, crossing his arms.

"To your assignment in New York," Daniel said, his eyes narrowing. "We've been waiting for your confirmation, but you've gone silent. What's going on?"

Emma, listening from just outside the room, felt her heart sink. New York? Assignment? What did this mean?

Ben took a deep breath, his jaw tightening. "Daniel, I'm not going to New York. I've decided to stay here, in Willow Creek."

Daniel's eyes widened in surprise, then narrowed with disapproval. "Stay here? Ben, this is the opportunity of a lifetime. A permanent position with *Explore* as our lead travel correspondent. It's what you've been working toward for years."

"I know," Ben said, his voice calm but firm. "But things have changed. I've found something here, something I don't want to walk away from."

Daniel shook his head, clearly frustrated. "Ben, think about what you're saying. You're going to throw away your career for... what, exactly? A small-town life? This isn't you."

"It is now," Ben replied, his voice steady. "I've made my decision, Daniel. I'm staying."

For a moment, there was silence. Then Daniel sighed, running a hand through his hair. "I can't believe this. But if that's your choice... I can't force you. Just know that once you walk away from this, there's no going back."

Ben nodded, his expression resolute. "I understand."

Daniel looked at him for a long moment, then finally nodded. "Alright, Ben. I'll let the board know. Good luck."

With that, Daniel turned and walked out of the house, leaving Ben standing there, his expression unreadable. Emma watched as Daniel's car drove away, a mixture of relief and anxiety swirling in her chest.

When Ben finally walked back outside, Emma met him halfway, searching his face for answers. "Ben, what was that about?"

Ben sighed, running a hand through his hair. "That was my boss. He came to offer me a permanent position with the magazine—based in New York."

Emma's heart clenched. "New York?"

"I turned it down," Ben said, his voice firm. "I'm staying here, Emma. With you."

Relief flooded Emma's chest, but it was quickly followed by concern. "Ben, are you sure? I don't want you to give up your dreams for me."

Ben reached out, cupping her face in his hands. "You are my dream, Emma. This life, this place—it's what I want now. I've made my choice, and I don't regret it."

Emma searched his eyes, finding only sincerity and love in their depths. "If you're sure, then I'm with you, Ben. All the way."

Ben smiled, pulling her into a warm embrace. "I'm sure, Emma. We're in this together."

As they stood there, holding each other close, Emma knew that no matter what challenges lay ahead, they would face them together. Their love was strong, and it would carry them through anything life threw their way.

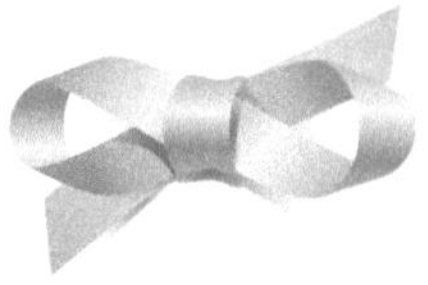

Chapter 9: Settling In

The days that followed Daniel Price's unexpected visit were a mix of relief and new beginnings for Emma and Ben. They continued to work on the house, but there was an unspoken understanding that things had shifted between them. Ben's decision to stay in Willow Creek wasn't just about the town; it was about building a life with Emma, and that realization brought them closer together.

As they painted the final coat on the living room walls, Emma glanced over at Ben, who was carefully trimming the edges. There was a peacefulness in his demeanor that hadn't been there before, a sense of contentment that made her heart swell with affection.

"Ben," Emma said, breaking the comfortable silence, "I know you've given up a lot to stay here, and I just want you to know how much it means to me. But if you ever have second thoughts, if you miss the life you had before—"

Ben cut her off, setting down his brush and walking over to her. He took her hands in his, his gaze steady and filled with love. "Emma, I don't have any second thoughts. What I had before doesn't compare to what I have now—with you. I've never been happier, and I don't want to be anywhere else."

Emma smiled, her worries melting away. "I just needed to hear you say that."

Ben leaned in and kissed her, a slow and tender kiss that conveyed everything words couldn't. When they finally pulled back, Emma felt a warmth spread through her, knowing that this was where they both belonged.

As they finished up their work for the day, the house slowly transformed into a home. The furniture they had selected together filled the space, and the rooms began to take on a cozy, lived-in feel. It wasn't just a house anymore—it was their home, a place where they could build a future together.

One evening, after a long day of working on the house, Ben and Emma decided to take a break and enjoy a quiet dinner at the bakery. Emma prepared a simple meal, and they set up a small table by the window, watching the sun set over the town square.

"This is nice," Ben said, taking a bite of the homemade stew Emma had prepared. "I could get used to this."

Emma smiled, enjoying the quiet intimacy of the moment. "Me too. It's like everything is falling into place."

Ben nodded, his expression thoughtful. "You know, I've been thinking about what's next. Now that the house is almost finished, I need to figure out what I'm going to do for work."

Emma looked at him, curious. "Have you thought about starting your own business? You could still write, but you'd be your own boss."

Ben considered her suggestion, a smile tugging at the corners of his mouth. "That's not a bad idea. I could focus on stories about small towns, travel destinations, and the people who make those places special. I could even feature Willow Creek as my first project."

Emma's eyes lit up with excitement. "I love that idea! And you could set up a small office in the house—something that's all yours."

Ben grinned, clearly warming to the idea. "I think I will. Thanks, Emma. You always know how to put things into perspective."

They continued to talk about their plans, the conversation flowing easily as they discussed the possibilities. It was clear that they were both excited about the future, about the life they were building together. The uncertainty that had once hung over them had been replaced with a sense of purpose and direction.

After dinner, they decided to take a walk through the town square. The festival had ended, but the autumn decorations still adorned the storefronts, and the air was filled with the scent of fallen leaves and wood smoke. As they strolled hand in hand, Emma felt a deep sense of contentment settle over her.

"This is perfect," Emma said softly, squeezing Ben's hand. "I don't think I've ever been this happy."

Ben smiled, pulling her close. "Me neither. It feels like everything I've been searching for has led me here—to you."

Emma leaned her head on his shoulder, feeling the steady beat of his heart. They walked in comfortable silence, the town around them quiet and peaceful. It was a moment of pure contentment, a glimpse of the life they would share in the years to come.

As they made their way back to the bakery, Emma realized that this was what she had always wanted—a life filled with love, companionship, and the simple joys of everyday moments. And now that she had found it with Ben, she knew she would never let it go.

When they reached the bakery, Ben paused at the door, turning to face her. "Emma, there's something I've been meaning to ask you."

Emma looked up at him, her heart skipping a beat. "What is it?"

Ben took a deep breath, his expression serious but tender. "Would you consider moving in with me? I know it's a big step, but it feels right. I want to wake up every day knowing you're by my side."

Emma's heart swelled with emotion, tears prickling at the corners of her eyes. "Yes, Ben. I'd love to move in with you."

Ben's face broke into a wide smile, and he pulled her into a tight embrace. "You've made me the happiest man in the world, Emma."

Emma laughed, her voice thick with emotion. "I'm pretty happy myself."

They stood there for a moment, holding each other close, the future stretching out before them filled with promise and hope. It was a new chapter in their lives, one they were eager to begin together.

As they walked inside, Emma knew that this was just the beginning. There would be challenges, of course, but they would face them together, as partners, as a team. And no matter what the future held, they would always have each other—and the life they were building in Willow Creek.

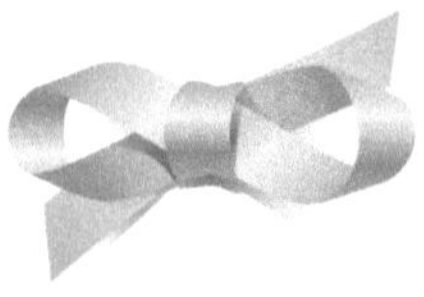

Chapter 10: A New Beginning

The next morning, Emma woke up in Ben's arms, the soft morning light filtering through the curtains of their newly finished bedroom. The house was quiet, with only the sound of their breathing and the distant chirping of birds breaking the stillness. For a moment, she simply lay there, soaking in the warmth and comfort of being so close to the man she loved.

As if sensing her thoughts, Ben stirred beside her, his arms tightening around her in a gentle embrace. "Good morning," he murmured, his voice husky with sleep.

"Good morning," Emma replied, her voice soft. She turned to face him, a smile tugging at her lips. "I still can't believe we're finally here, in our home."

Ben smiled back, brushing a strand of hair from her face. "Neither can I. But it feels right, doesn't it? Like this is exactly where we're meant to be."

Emma nodded, feeling a deep sense of contentment. "It does. And I'm so excited for everything that's ahead—for us."

Ben's expression grew more serious as he looked into her eyes. "Me too, Emma. I want to make this life with you, every day, for as long as we both shall live."

Emma's breath caught at the gravity of his words, and for a moment, she couldn't speak. There was something in his tone, in the way he was looking at her, that made her heart race. She had known for some time that their relationship was serious, but this felt like a declaration of something even deeper—something permanent.

Ben reached out and took her hand, his gaze never leaving hers. "Emma, I know we haven't been together for very long, but I've never been more certain of anything in my life. I love you, and I want to spend the rest of my life with you. Will you marry me?"

The question hung in the air, and for a moment, Emma couldn't breathe. Tears welled up in her eyes, and she felt a flood of emotions—joy, love, hope—all swirling together in a dizzying rush.

"Yes," she whispered, her voice trembling with emotion. "Yes, Ben, I'll marry you."

Ben's face broke into a wide, relieved smile, and he pulled her into his arms, holding her tightly. "You've made me the happiest man in the world, Emma," he murmured into her hair. "I promise I'll spend the rest of my life making you just as happy."

Emma laughed through her tears, the sound filled with pure, unfiltered joy. "I already am, Ben. I already am."

They spent the morning wrapped in each other's arms, talking about their future and what it would look like now that they were engaged. The house, which had once been just a project, was now their home, the place where they would build their life together as husband and wife.

Later that day, Emma and Ben decided to share the news with their friends in town. They started at the bakery, where Emma knew the regulars would be gathering for their usual morning coffee and pastries. As they walked in, hand in hand, the warm scent of cinnamon and sugar filled the air, and Emma felt a renewed sense of belonging.

Mabel, the town's most avid gossip, was the first to notice them. "Well, look who's finally decided to show up!" she called out, her eyes twinkling with mischief. "And what's this? You two look like you're glowing!"

Emma exchanged a glance with Ben, who gave her a nod of encouragement. She took a deep breath and smiled. "We have some news," she announced, her voice clear and confident. "Ben and I are engaged!"

There was a brief moment of stunned silence before the room erupted into cheers and congratulations. Emma found herself wrapped in a whirlwind of hugs, handshakes, and well-wishes, her heart swelling with love for the community that had always been her home.

Mabel, of course, was the most enthusiastic, pulling Emma into a tight embrace. "Oh, my dear, I knew this was coming! You two are just perfect for each other. I can't wait to see the wedding—you're going to be the most beautiful bride!"

Emma blushed, feeling overwhelmed but incredibly happy. "Thank you, Mabel. We're still figuring out the details, but I promise we'll keep everyone in the loop."

As the excitement died down and the regulars returned to their seats, Emma and Ben were approached by Mrs. Thompson, the elderly woman who had been a regular at the bakery for as long as Emma could remember. She smiled up at them, her eyes twinkling with wisdom and warmth.

"I'm so happy for you both," Mrs. Thompson said, her voice gentle. "Marriage is a beautiful journey, and I can see that you two are going to have a wonderful life together. Just remember to always be each other's best friend, no matter what life throws your way."

Emma felt a lump form in her throat at the sincerity of Mrs. Thompson's words. "Thank you, Mrs. Thompson. That means a lot to us."

Ben nodded in agreement, his hand resting on the small of Emma's back. "We'll do our best to live up to that advice."

After spending some time at the bakery, they continued their rounds through town, sharing the news with other friends and neighbors. Everywhere they went, they were met with smiles, congratulations, and offers of help with the wedding planning. It was clear that the town was as excited about their engagement as they were.

As the day came to a close, Emma and Ben returned home, tired but happy. They sat together on the porch, watching the sun set over the trees, the sky ablaze with shades of orange and pink.

"I can't believe we're really getting married," Emma said, her voice filled with wonder. "It feels like a dream."

Ben smiled, his gaze fixed on her. "It's real, Emma. And I can't wait to spend the rest of my life with you."

Emma leaned her head on his shoulder, feeling a deep sense of peace settle over her. "Neither can I, Ben. Neither can I."

As the stars began to twinkle overhead, they sat in comfortable silence, content in the knowledge that they had found something rare and precious—true love, the kind that could weather any storm and shine brighter with every passing day.

Chapter 11: Wedding Plans and Unexpected Visitors

The days following Emma and Ben's engagement announcement were filled with excitement and a flurry of activity. It seemed as though the entire town of Willow Creek was abuzz with wedding fever. Everywhere they went, people offered their congratulations, and many eagerly volunteered their services for the upcoming wedding.

Emma was touched by the outpouring of support, but as the reality of planning a wedding began to sink in, she couldn't help but feel a little overwhelmed. There were so many decisions to be made—where to hold the ceremony, what kind of dress to wear, who to invite. It was all a bit daunting, and she found herself wishing for a simpler way to celebrate their love.

One crisp autumn morning, as Emma sat at the kitchen table with a notebook filled with ideas and a cup of tea, Ben walked in, looking as relaxed as ever. He had just returned from a morning jog and was clearly in high spirits.

"Good morning, beautiful," Ben said, leaning down to give her a quick kiss. "How's the planning going?"

Emma sighed, running a hand through her hair. "It's going... okay. There's just so much to think about. I want our wedding to be special, but I also don't want to get caught up in all the details and lose sight of what really matters."

Ben sat down beside her, taking her hand in his. "You're right, Emma. The most important thing is that we're getting married. The rest is just icing on the cake. If it's too stressful, we can keep it simple. It doesn't have to be a big event unless that's what you want."

Emma looked into his eyes, feeling a wave of gratitude for how understanding and supportive he was. "I think keeping it simple might be best. Maybe something outdoors, with just our closest friends and family. What do you think?"

Ben smiled, clearly relieved. "I love that idea. Something intimate, where we can focus on what's really important—our commitment to each other."

Emma nodded, feeling a weight lift off her shoulders. "I'll start making a list of possible locations. Maybe somewhere by the river? It's where we really connected, after all."

"That sounds perfect," Ben agreed. "We can go check out some spots later today, see what feels right."

As they talked, a sense of peace settled over Emma. The decision to keep the wedding simple felt right, like it was in line with who they were as a couple. They didn't need anything grand or elaborate—just a beautiful day surrounded by the people they loved.

Later that afternoon, they set out to explore the areas around the river, looking for the perfect spot to hold their ceremony. The autumn leaves crunched underfoot as they walked, and the air was crisp and cool, filled with the earthy scent of the season.

They eventually found a small clearing near the water, where the trees formed a natural archway overhead. The sunlight filtered through the branches, casting a warm, golden glow over the space. It was quiet, serene, and utterly perfect.

"This is it," Emma said, her voice filled with awe. "This is where I want to marry you, Ben."

Ben took her hand, squeezing it gently. "Then this is where it will be. I can't imagine a more beautiful place to start our life together."

With the location settled, Emma felt a renewed sense of excitement about the wedding. The simplicity of it all felt right, like they were honoring their love in the most genuine way possible.

But just as they were about to head back to town, their peaceful moment was interrupted by the sound of footsteps behind them. They turned to see a woman approaching, her expression one of surprise and delight.

"Emma? Ben? Is that really you?" the woman called out, her voice filled with warmth.

Emma squinted, trying to place the familiar face. As the woman came closer, recognition dawned. "Alyssa? What are you doing here?"

Alyssa Reynolds had been Emma's best friend in college, but they had lost touch over the years as life had taken them in different directions. Seeing her now, in Willow Creek of all places, was a complete shock.

"I was in the area for work and decided to take a detour through Willow Creek," Alyssa explained, her eyes wide with excitement. "I can't believe I ran into you like this! It's been years!"

Emma laughed, still trying to process the coincidence. "It really has. It's so good to see you, Alyssa. What brings you to a small town like ours?"

Alyssa glanced around, her expression softening as she took in the beauty of the surroundings. "I needed a break from the city, a chance to clear my head. And, well... something drew me here. I didn't expect to find you, though!"

Ben stepped forward, offering his hand with a friendly smile. "I'm Ben, by the way. Emma's fiancé."

Alyssa's eyes widened with surprise and then joy. "Fiancé? Oh my gosh, Emma, that's amazing! Congratulations!"

Emma blushed, feeling a little self-conscious. "Thank you. We're actually planning our wedding right now—out here by the river."

Alyssa looked around, her smile growing wider. "This place is perfect. I'm so happy for you, Emma. You deserve all the happiness in the world."

Emma felt a rush of affection for her old friend. "Thank you, Alyssa. I'm really glad you're here. How long are you staying?"

"I was only planning to be here for a couple of days, but now... I don't know," Alyssa admitted, her tone thoughtful. "Maybe I'll stick around a bit longer. It feels good to be here, with you."

Emma exchanged a glance with Ben, who nodded in understanding. "You're welcome to stay as long as you like," Emma said warmly. "It'll be like old times."

As they walked back to town, catching up on the years they had missed, Emma couldn't help but feel that Alyssa's unexpected arrival was more than just a coincidence. It felt like fate, bringing an old friend back into her life at just the right moment.

With the wedding plans moving forward and Alyssa by her side, Emma felt that everything was falling into place. The future was bright, filled with love, friendship, and the promise of a beautiful life with Ben.

Chapter 12: Old Friends, New Beginnings

Alyssa's unexpected arrival brought a new dynamic into Emma and Ben's life. The old friends quickly fell back into an easy rhythm, spending hours reminiscing about their college days and catching up on all that had happened since. For Emma, having Alyssa around felt like rediscovering a piece of herself she hadn't realized was missing.

As the days passed, Alyssa settled comfortably into Willow Creek, charmed by the town's warmth and the simple pleasures of small-town life. She helped Emma with wedding plans, offering fresh ideas and a calming presence that kept Emma from getting overwhelmed. Ben, too, quickly grew fond of Alyssa, appreciating her wit and the positive energy she brought into their lives.

One afternoon, as the three of them sat around the kitchen table with cups of tea, poring over ideas for the wedding, Alyssa suddenly grew quiet. She seemed lost in thought, her fingers tracing the rim of her cup.

"Alyssa, is something on your mind?" Emma asked, noticing the change in her friend's demeanor.

Alyssa looked up, her expression pensive. "Actually, there is. I've been thinking a lot since I got here... about my life, my career. Everything, really."

Emma exchanged a concerned glance with Ben before turning back to Alyssa. "What's going on? You know you can talk to us."

Alyssa sighed, setting her cup down. "I've been living in the city for so long, chasing career goals that, in the end, don't seem to matter as much as I thought they would. Coming here, seeing you and Ben, and feeling the sense of community in this town... it's made me realize how much I've been missing."

Emma reached out and placed a hand on Alyssa's. "What are you thinking of doing?"

Alyssa hesitated, then gave a small, determined smile. "I think I need a change. Maybe it's time to leave the city behind and find something that brings me real happiness. I've been inspired by what you and Ben have here. It's made me realize that I want more out of life than just a career."

Ben nodded in understanding. "Sometimes, it takes stepping away from everything you know to find out what you really want."

Alyssa looked at him, her eyes reflecting a mixture of gratitude and uncertainty. "That's exactly it. And being here, with you two... it feels like I've been given a second chance to figure out what that is."

Emma smiled, her heart swelling with affection for her friend. "You're always welcome here, Alyssa. If you want to stay in Willow Creek, you can. There's no rush to figure everything out."

Alyssa's smile widened, and she looked around the cozy kitchen, as if seeing it through new eyes. "You know, I think I'd like that. Maybe I'll stay for a while and see where life takes me."

The decision was made, and with it came a renewed sense of excitement. Alyssa threw herself into helping Emma and Ben with their wedding plans, and the three of them spent their days exploring the town, meeting new people, and enjoying the simple pleasures of small-town life.

As they worked together, Emma noticed how naturally Alyssa fit into their lives. It was as if she had always been there, a part of their story that had finally found its way back. And as they grew closer, Emma couldn't help but wonder if Alyssa's arrival was part of something bigger—another piece of the puzzle that was their life together.

One evening, after a particularly productive day of wedding planning, the three of them decided to take a break and enjoy a quiet dinner at the local diner. The place was bustling with activity, the warm glow of the lights reflecting off the polished wood tables. The scent of comfort food filled the air, and the hum of conversation created a cozy, welcoming atmosphere.

As they settled into a booth, the waitress, a friendly woman named Linda, approached with a warm smile. "Well, if it isn't our newest residents! How are you three doing tonight?"

"We're doing great, Linda," Emma replied, returning the smile. "Just taking a break from wedding planning."

Linda's eyes twinkled with excitement. "I heard about that! The whole town's buzzing with the news. Everyone's so happy for you two."

"Thanks, Linda," Ben said, glancing at Emma with a loving smile. "We're pretty excited ourselves."

As they placed their orders and waited for their food, the conversation turned to the future. Alyssa shared her thoughts on what she might do next, from exploring new career options to possibly starting her own business. Emma and Ben offered their support and encouragement, knowing that whatever Alyssa chose, she would excel.

When their food arrived, they ate and talked, the easy camaraderie between them making the evening feel like one of those perfect moments that would be remembered for years to come. Emma felt a deep sense of contentment as she looked around the table, grateful for the love and friendship that surrounded her.

After dinner, they walked back to the house under the light of a full moon, the cool night air crisp and refreshing. The conversation was lighter now, filled with laughter and teasing as they strolled through the quiet streets of Willow Creek.

As they reached the house, Ben paused, looking up at the sky. "It's a beautiful night," he said, his voice thoughtful. "It reminds me of why I love it here so much."

Emma wrapped her arm around his, leaning into him. "It really is. There's something magical about this place, about the life we're building here."

Alyssa smiled, her eyes reflecting the same contentment. "You're right. This place... it feels like home."

They stood there for a moment, taking in the beauty of the night and the warmth of each other's company. It was a simple, perfect moment, one that captured everything Emma had ever wanted—love, friendship, and the promise of a bright future.

As they headed inside, Emma knew that whatever challenges lay ahead, they would face them together. With Ben by her side and Alyssa as a cherished part of their lives, she felt ready to take on anything.

And as she drifted off to sleep that night, Emma dreamed of the life they were creating—a life filled with love, laughter, and the unshakable belief that they had found something truly special in each other.

Chapter 13: The Wedding Date

As the days in Willow Creek grew shorter and the crispness of late autumn settled in, Emma and Ben's wedding plans began to take shape. With Alyssa's help, they finalized the details, and the excitement of their upcoming nuptials buzzed in the air like a gentle current.

One morning, as Emma and Ben sat together at the kitchen table, sipping their coffee and going over the final guest list, the conversation turned to an important decision they had yet to make.

"We've got the location, the guests, and most of the details ironed out," Ben said, tapping the pen against the edge of the table. "But we haven't set a date yet."

Emma looked at him, her heart skipping a beat. The date—it was the final piece that would make everything feel real. "You're right. We need to pick a day that's special to us, something that feels right."

Ben nodded, his eyes thoughtful. "What about a date in late November? The autumn colors will still be around, and it gives us time to make sure everything's perfect."

Emma considered this, a smile tugging at her lips. "That sounds lovely. I've always loved the idea of an autumn wedding. How about November 21st? It's a Saturday, and it's close enough to Thanksgiving that our friends and family could stay and celebrate with us through the holiday."

Ben's smile widened. "November 21st it is, then. It's perfect."

Emma's heart fluttered with excitement as she wrote the date at the top of the guest list. Seeing it there, in black and white, made it all feel so real. In just a few short weeks, she would be marrying the man she loved, surrounded by the people who meant the most to them.

As the wedding date was set, the preparations kicked into high gear. The small clearing by the river where they had chosen to hold the ceremony was transformed with the help of the town's residents, who pitched in to make it beautiful. The trees were adorned with twinkling fairy lights, and rustic wooden benches were set up for the guests. It was simple, elegant, and utterly perfect.

Alyssa proved to be an invaluable help, not only with the wedding details but also with keeping Emma grounded and calm. They spent their afternoons crafting decorations, baking treats, and laughing about old times. It was as if no time had passed since their college days, and the bond between them only grew stronger.

One evening, as they were finishing up a batch of cookies for the reception, Alyssa turned to Emma, her expression serious. "Emma, I need to ask you something."

Emma paused, looking up from the tray of cookies. "What is it, Alyssa?"

Alyssa took a deep breath, her voice softening. "Would you mind if I stayed in Willow Creek for a while longer? I know I came here on a whim, but this place... it feels like home. I think I need to figure out what's next for me, and being here with you and Ben, it feels right."

Emma's heart swelled with affection. "Alyssa, I'd love for you to stay. You're always welcome here, for as long as you want."

Alyssa's smile was full of gratitude. "Thank you, Emma. I've been so happy here. It's been a long time since I felt this way."

Emma reached out and squeezed her friend's hand. "You belong here, Alyssa. I'm so glad you came back into my life."

As the days passed and the wedding drew closer, everything seemed to fall into place. The dresses were chosen, the vows were written, and the final touches were added to the ceremony site. The town of Willow Creek buzzed with excitement, and it seemed as though everyone was looking forward to the big day.

On the eve of the wedding, Emma found herself unable to sleep. She lay in bed, staring up at the ceiling, her mind racing with anticipation. She was excited, of course, but there was also a nervous energy thrumming through her, a sense that everything was about to change.

Unable to lie still any longer, Emma quietly slipped out of bed and made her way to the living room. The house was silent, the only sound the soft ticking of the clock on the mantle. She wrapped herself in a blanket and sat on the couch, staring out the window at the moonlit night.

A few moments later, she heard soft footsteps and turned to see Ben standing in the doorway, his hair tousled from sleep. "Can't sleep?" he asked, his voice gentle.

Emma shook her head, smiling a little. "Too many thoughts running through my head, I guess."

Ben walked over and sat beside her, wrapping an arm around her shoulders. "Nervous?"

"A little," Emma admitted. "But mostly, I'm just excited. It's all happening so fast, and I can't wait to start this new chapter with you."

Ben pressed a kiss to her temple, his touch reassuring. "I know what you mean. But we're in this together, Emma. Whatever comes our way, we'll face it side by side."

Emma leaned into him, feeling the steady beat of his heart against her. "I know. And that's what makes everything feel right."

They sat there in comfortable silence for a while, just holding each other and soaking in the quiet moments before the whirlwind of the wedding day began. The uncertainty that had once filled Emma's heart had been replaced with a deep sense of peace, a knowing that she was exactly where she was meant to be—with Ben, in the life they were building together.

As dawn approached, Ben stood, pulling Emma to her feet. "We should try to get some sleep. Tomorrow's going to be a big day."

Emma nodded, a smile tugging at her lips. "You're right. And it's going to be perfect."

With one last kiss, they headed back to bed, knowing that when they woke, it would be the day that would change their lives forever.

Chapter 14: The Wedding Day

The morning of November 21st dawned crisp and clear, the sky a brilliant blue with just a hint of autumn's fading warmth. Emma woke up to the sound of birds chirping outside her window, a sense of calm washing over her as she realized that today was the day she would marry Ben.

She stretched lazily, a smile spreading across her face as the realization fully sank in. Today was her wedding day. She had dreamed about this moment for so long, and now that it was finally here, it felt like everything had fallen perfectly into place.

Downstairs, the house was already bustling with activity. Alyssa and a few of Emma's closest friends were busy preparing for the day, their laughter and chatter filling the air with excitement. When Emma stepped into the kitchen, she was greeted with cheers and hugs, her friends pulling her into the joyful whirlwind of final preparations.

"Good morning, bride-to-be!" Alyssa exclaimed, handing Emma a cup of tea. "How are you feeling?"

Emma took a sip of the warm tea, her smile widening. "I'm feeling amazing. I can't believe it's finally here."

Alyssa beamed, her eyes shining with happiness. "You're going to be the most beautiful bride, Emma. Everything is ready, and it's going to be perfect."

The morning passed in a blur of activity as Emma and her friends got ready. The small house was filled with the scent of flowers and the sound of music as they laughed and shared stories. Emma's dress, a simple yet elegant gown that perfectly suited the rustic charm of the outdoor setting, hung on a nearby hook, waiting for the moment when she would finally step into it.

As the time drew closer, Emma found herself growing more excited with each passing minute. The nervousness that had kept her awake the night before had vanished, replaced by a deep sense of peace and certainty. This was her day, her moment, and she was ready to embrace it with all her heart.

When it was finally time to get dressed, Alyssa helped Emma into her gown, her fingers gentle as she fastened the buttons down the back. Emma stood in front of the mirror, her breath catching in her throat as she took in the sight of herself. The dress was perfect, the soft fabric flowing around her like a whisper, and the way it hugged her curves made her feel beautiful in a way she never had before.

"You look stunning," Alyssa said, her voice filled with emotion. "Ben is going to lose his mind when he sees you."

Emma laughed softly, her eyes shining with tears of happiness. "I hope so."

With her hair pinned up in soft waves and a simple veil draped over her shoulders, Emma was ready. She took a deep breath, her heart racing with anticipation, and nodded to Alyssa. "Let's do this."

The ceremony site by the river was even more beautiful than Emma had imagined. The trees, still adorned with their golden and orange leaves, formed a natural archway over the path leading to the clearing. The fairy lights twinkled in the branches, casting a soft, magical glow over the entire area. The wooden benches were filled with friends and family, all of whom rose to their feet as Emma stepped onto the path.

Her heart swelled with emotion as she walked down the aisle, her eyes locked on Ben, who stood waiting for her at the end. He looked as handsome as ever in a tailored suit, but it was the expression on his face that took her breath away—pure, unfiltered love, shining in his eyes as he watched her approach.

When she finally reached him, Ben took her hands in his, his touch warm and steady. "You're breathtaking, Emma," he whispered, his voice thick with emotion.

"So are you," Emma replied, her voice trembling with happiness.

The ceremony was simple, heartfelt, and perfect. They exchanged vows that they had written themselves, promises that reflected the love and commitment they had found in each other. There wasn't a dry eye in the clearing as they spoke the words that would bind them together for the rest of their lives.

When the officiant finally pronounced them husband and wife, Emma felt a surge of joy unlike anything she had ever experienced. Ben leaned in, cupping her face in his hands, and kissed her with all the love and passion that had brought them to this moment. The crowd erupted into cheers, and Emma knew that this was the beginning of the rest of their lives.

The reception that followed was a celebration of love, friendship, and community. The small town of Willow Creek had come together to make the day special, and it showed in every detail—from the homemade food to the music that filled the air. Emma and Ben danced under the stars, surrounded by the people who had supported them from the beginning, and it was a night filled with laughter, joy, and the kind of memories that would last a lifetime.

As the evening drew to a close, Emma and Ben stood by the river, watching the reflection of the moon on the water. The night was quiet now, the festivities winding down, and they were finally alone, just the two of them.

"This day has been perfect," Emma said softly, leaning her head on Ben's shoulder. "I couldn't have asked for anything more."

Ben wrapped his arm around her, pulling her close. "It was perfect because I married you. Everything else was just icing on the cake."

Emma smiled, her heart full to bursting. "I love you, Ben. I can't wait to see what the future holds for us."

"Neither can I," Ben replied, pressing a kiss to her temple. "But whatever it is, we'll face it together."

They stood there for a long time, wrapped in each other's arms, watching the river flow gently by. The future stretched out before them, filled with endless possibilities, and Emma knew that as long as they had each other, everything would be exactly as it should be.

Chapter 15: The Honeymoon Phase

The days following the wedding were a blissful blur for Emma and Ben. They had decided to spend their honeymoon in Willow Creek, opting for a simple, quiet celebration of their new life together rather than a big trip. The town had become their sanctuary, a place where they could focus on each other and the future they were building.

Each day, they explored the town and its surroundings, finding new places to visit and creating memories that would last a lifetime. They spent long afternoons by the river, picnicking under the trees, and quiet evenings at home, curled up together by the fire. It was everything Emma had ever dreamed of—pure, uncomplicated happiness.

One morning, about a week after the wedding, Ben surprised Emma with a plan to visit a nearby vineyard that was known for its beautiful scenery and excellent wine. It was a place neither of them had been before, and the idea of exploring it together excited Emma.

They set off after breakfast, the autumn sun warm on their faces as they drove through the rolling hills outside of Willow Creek. The vineyard was nestled in a valley, surrounded by rows of grapevines that stretched out as far as the eye could see. The colors of the leaves, deep reds, and golden yellows, created a stunning contrast against the clear blue sky.

As they arrived, they were greeted by the vineyard's owner, a friendly man named Carlo, who welcomed them warmly and offered to give them a personal tour. Carlo led them through the vineyard, explaining the process of winemaking and sharing stories of the land and its history. It was fascinating, and Emma found herself enchanted by the beauty of the place and the passion with which Carlo spoke.

After the tour, they sat on the terrace overlooking the vineyard, sampling a selection of wines paired with local cheeses and bread. The flavors were rich and complex, each sip and bite a new experience. But as wonderful as the wine and food were, it was the simple pleasure of being together that made the day so special.

"This place is incredible," Emma said, leaning back in her chair and gazing out over the vineyard. "I'm so glad you brought me here, Ben."

Ben smiled, reaching across the table to take her hand. "I wanted to do something special for you. We've both been so busy with the wedding and settling into married life, and I thought it would be nice to just get away for a day, just the two of us."

Emma's heart swelled with love for him. "You always know exactly what I need. This has been perfect."

They spent the rest of the afternoon at the vineyard, strolling through the rows of vines and enjoying the peacefulness of the countryside. As the sun began to set, casting a golden glow over the landscape, they made their way back to the terrace, where Carlo had prepared a small table with a bottle of their favorite wine from the tasting.

"To us," Ben said, lifting his glass as they sat down. "To this life we're building together, one day at a time."

Emma clinked her glass against his, her smile warm and content. "To us."

As they sipped their wine and watched the sun dip below the horizon, Emma felt a deep sense of contentment. This was what she had always wanted—a life filled with love, simple pleasures, and the kind of moments that would stay with her forever.

But as the evening grew darker and the stars began to twinkle in the sky, Emma couldn't shake the feeling that something was on Ben's mind. He had been quiet for a while, his gaze distant as he stared out at the vineyard.

"Ben, is everything okay?" Emma asked gently, placing her hand on his arm.

Ben blinked, snapping out of his thoughts, and turned to her with a reassuring smile. "Everything's fine, Emma. I was just thinking about how lucky I am to have you in my life."

Emma studied his face, sensing there was more he wasn't saying. "You know you can talk to me about anything, right? Whatever it is, we'll figure it out together."

Ben's smile softened, and he nodded. "I know, Emma. And I promise, everything's fine. I'm just... reflecting on how much has changed in such a short time. It's overwhelming in the best way possible."

Emma squeezed his hand, understanding his feelings. They had been through so much in the past few months, and it was only natural that he would need time to process everything. "It has been a whirlwind, hasn't it? But I wouldn't change a thing."

"Neither would I," Ben agreed, his expression lightening. "And I'm so excited for everything that's ahead of us."

They finished their wine and began the drive back to Willow Creek, the night air cool and refreshing as it streamed through the open windows. The quiet of the road and the steady rhythm of the car's engine lulled them into a comfortable silence, each lost in their thoughts but connected by the bond they shared.

When they arrived home, Ben parked the car and turned to Emma with a serious expression. "Emma, there's something I've been thinking about. Something I want us to talk about."

Emma's heart skipped a beat, her curiosity piqued. "What is it, Ben?"

Ben hesitated for a moment, then took a deep breath. "I've been thinking about starting a family. I know we've just gotten married, but I can't stop imagining what it would be like to have a little one running around, someone we can love and raise together."

Emma's breath caught in her throat. The idea of having a family with Ben was something she had dreamed about, but hearing him say it out loud made it feel so real. "You really want that?"

"I do," Ben said, his voice steady and filled with emotion. "But only if you're ready, Emma. There's no rush. I just wanted to share what's been on my mind."

Emma smiled, her heart swelling with love. "I want that too, Ben. I've always dreamed of having a family with you. Maybe we should start thinking about it."

Ben's eyes lit up with happiness, and he leaned over to kiss her, his touch filled with love and promise. "I'm so glad to hear that, Emma. Whatever happens, we'll figure it out together."

As they walked into the house, hand in hand, Emma felt a sense of anticipation building within her. The future was wide open, filled with possibilities, and she couldn't wait to see where their journey would take them next.

Chapter 16: Dreams of Tomorrow

The days after their conversation about starting a family were filled with a new sense of excitement and anticipation for both Emma and Ben. They continued to enjoy the simple pleasures of their honeymoon phase, but now, there was an added layer of hope for the future they were planning together.

One evening, as they sat by the fire in their cozy living room, Emma brought up the topic again. She had been thinking about it a lot, and she wanted to make sure they were on the same page.

"Ben," she began, looking over at him as he sipped his tea, "I've been thinking more about what we talked about the other night—about starting a family."

Ben set his cup down and turned to her, his expression attentive. "I've been thinking about it too. What's on your mind?"

Emma took a deep breath, choosing her words carefully. "I want to make sure we're both ready for this. I know it's something we both want, but it's a big step, and I want to be sure we're prepared—emotionally, financially, in every way."

Ben nodded, his eyes serious but understanding. "I completely agree. It's a huge responsibility, and I want to make sure we're ready too. But I also believe that we'll never feel completely 'ready' in the traditional sense. I think it's more about being ready to embrace the unknown, to face whatever challenges come our way together."

Emma smiled, reassured by his words. "You're right. We've always faced everything together, and we'll do the same with this. I just... I want to make sure we're giving our future children the best life we can."

"And we will," Ben said, taking her hand in his. "We've built a strong foundation, Emma. We have a home, a community that supports us, and most importantly, we have each other. That's more than a lot of people start with."

Emma felt a wave of love and gratitude for Ben wash over her. "You always know how to make me feel better. I'm so lucky to have you."

Ben smiled, leaning in to kiss her gently. "I'm the lucky one, Emma. And whatever comes next, we'll figure it out together."

They spent the rest of the evening discussing their hopes and dreams for the future, imagining what their life might look like with a child in it. They talked about everything from what kind of parents they wanted to be to the values they hoped to instill in their children. It was a conversation filled with love, hope, and the deep bond they shared.

As the weeks passed, Emma and Ben began to take small steps toward making their dream a reality. They didn't rush into anything, but they started to prepare in subtle ways—saving more money, making small changes to their home to make it more family-friendly, and talking about what life might look like when they were ready to take that next step.

In the meantime, life in Willow Creek continued to be as warm and welcoming as ever. The town had fully embraced Ben and Emma as a couple, and now, as newlyweds, they were often the subject of well-wishes and congratulations from everyone they met. Alyssa, who had become a permanent fixture in their lives, was also thriving in the small town. She had found a job at the local bookstore, where she quickly became a beloved part of the community.

One crisp autumn afternoon, Emma, Ben, and Alyssa decided to take a walk through the town square, which was still adorned with the remnants of the harvest festival. The air was filled with the scent of cinnamon and wood smoke, and the leaves crunched beneath their feet as they strolled through the quiet streets.

"This place has really become home, hasn't it?" Alyssa said, her voice filled with contentment as she looked around.

"It really has," Emma agreed, linking her arm with Alyssa's. "I'm so glad you decided to stay. It wouldn't be the same without you."

Alyssa smiled, squeezing Emma's arm. "I can't imagine being anywhere else. And I'm so excited for what the future holds—for all of us."

They continued their walk, the conversation light and filled with laughter. As they passed the local park, they noticed a group of children playing, their joyful voices echoing through the air. Emma paused, watching them with a soft smile, her thoughts drifting to the possibility of one day having a child of her own.

Ben noticed her thoughtful expression and wrapped an arm around her shoulders. "You're thinking about it, aren't you?"

Emma nodded, leaning into him. "I am. It's hard not to when I see how happy they are. I can't wait to experience that with you, Ben."

"And we will," Ben said, his voice filled with quiet certainty. "When the time is right, it will happen."

Emma smiled, feeling a sense of peace settle over her. She knew that their journey to parenthood would happen when it was meant to, and in the meantime, she was content to enjoy every moment of the life they were building together.

As they continued their walk, Emma felt a deep sense of gratitude for the life she had. She had a loving husband, a wonderful friend in Alyssa, and a community that supported and cared for her. The future was filled with possibilities, and she knew that whatever came next, she would face it with love, hope, and the unwavering belief that she was exactly where she was meant to be.

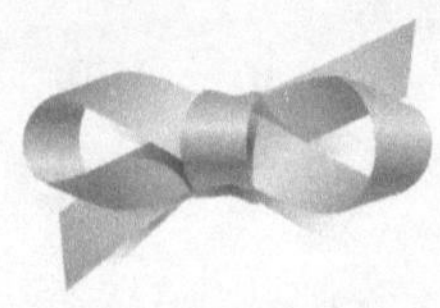

Chapter 17: A New Chapter Begins

As the weeks turned into months, winter began to settle over Willow Creek. The first snowfall of the season dusted the town in a blanket of white, transforming the landscape into a picturesque winter wonderland. Emma and Ben embraced the change in season, finding joy in the quiet beauty of the snow-covered streets and the cozy warmth of their home.

Life in Willow Creek slowed down as the cold weather set in, but for Emma and Ben, it was a time of reflection and planning for the future. They spent long evenings by the fire, discussing their hopes and dreams, and making plans for the coming year. The idea of starting a family had taken root, and while they weren't rushing into anything, they were both excited about the possibilities.

One evening, as they sat together on the couch, wrapped in a blanket and sipping hot cocoa, Ben brought up a topic they hadn't yet discussed in detail.

"Emma, I've been thinking about something," Ben said, his tone thoughtful as he looked over at her.

Emma set her mug down and turned to him, curiosity piqued. "What's on your mind?"

"I've been thinking about our future—about starting a family and what that will look like for us," Ben began, his voice steady. "I know we've talked about it in broad terms, but I think it's time we start thinking about what steps we need to take to make it happen."

Emma nodded, understanding the seriousness of the conversation. "You're right. It's one thing to talk about it, but it's another to actually start planning. What are you thinking?"

Ben took a deep breath, choosing his words carefully. "I think we should start by making sure we're in the best place possible—physically, emotionally, and financially. We've already made some changes, but maybe we could take it a step further. We could both get check-ups, start saving more aggressively, and maybe even talk to a financial advisor to make sure we're on track."

Emma appreciated Ben's practical approach. "That sounds like a good plan. I want to make sure we're as prepared as we can be, too. And I like the idea of taking it one step at a time."

Ben smiled, reaching out to take her hand. "I'm glad you're on board. I know it's a lot to think about, but I want us to feel confident and ready when the time comes."

Emma squeezed his hand, feeling a surge of love for him. "We've always faced everything together, Ben. This is just the next chapter in our journey."

As they continued to talk, the conversation shifted to more immediate concerns—like preparing their home for the winter months and making sure they were stocked up on supplies. The snowfall had been light so far, but in Willow Creek, winter storms were always a possibility, and they wanted to be ready.

Over the next few days, they worked together to winterize the house, checking the insulation, sealing windows, and making sure the heating system was in top shape. It was a practical task, but as they worked side by side, it only reinforced the strong partnership they had built. They were a team, and they approached everything with the same sense of shared responsibility and care.

One afternoon, as they finished up their work, they decided to take a break and go for a walk through the snowy woods behind their house. The air was crisp and cold, their breath visible in the frosty air as they strolled along the quiet path. The world around them was still and peaceful, the only sound the crunch of snow beneath their boots.

"This is beautiful," Emma said, taking in the serene landscape. "I love winter in Willow Creek."

Ben nodded, his eyes scanning the snow-covered trees. "There's something magical about it, isn't there? It's like the whole world is holding its breath, waiting for something."

They walked in comfortable silence for a while, simply enjoying the beauty of the moment. As they rounded a bend in the path, they came across a small clearing where the trees opened up to reveal a frozen pond, its surface smooth and glistening in the late afternoon light.

Ben paused, a smile tugging at the corners of his mouth. "Do you remember when we talked about skating on a frozen pond? I think we might have just found the perfect spot."

Emma laughed, remembering the conversation they had had early in their relationship. "I do remember! I never thought we'd actually find a place like this."

Ben reached for her hand, his eyes twinkling with mischief. "What do you say? Should we come back tomorrow with our skates and give it a try?"

Emma's eyes lit up with excitement. "I'd love that. It sounds like the perfect winter adventure."

They stood there for a while longer, taking in the beauty of the frozen pond and the quiet of the woods around them. It was moments like these that made Emma feel so connected to Ben, so grateful for the life they were building together. Every day brought new experiences, new memories, and the promise of a future filled with love and joy.

As they headed back to the house, the sun dipping low on the horizon, Emma felt a sense of contentment settle over her. The world around them might be cold and still, but their hearts were warm, filled with the love they had for each other and the dreams they were nurturing together.

Chapter 18: Skating on Thin Ice

The following morning, Emma and Ben woke up early, excited about their plan to skate on the frozen pond. The sun was just beginning to rise, casting a soft pink glow over the snow-covered landscape. The world outside their window looked like a winter postcard, serene and beautiful.

Emma dressed warmly in layers, pulling on her thickest wool socks and lacing up her sturdy boots. She could feel the excitement bubbling up inside her as she rummaged through the closet to find their old ice skates, which had been tucked away since they moved in.

Ben joined her in the hallway, already bundled up in a warm coat and scarf. "Found them?" he asked, his eyes twinkling with anticipation.

"Yep, they were right where we left them," Emma replied, holding up the skates. "I can't wait to get out there."

After a quick breakfast of hot oatmeal and coffee, they grabbed their skates and set off for the pond. The air was crisp and cold, their breath forming little clouds as they walked through the woods. The snow crunched underfoot, the trees standing silent and tall around them, creating a peaceful and almost magical atmosphere.

When they reached the clearing, the pond looked just as perfect as it had the day before. The surface was smooth and glistening, reflecting the pale morning sky. Ben walked out onto the ice first, testing it carefully with his weight.

"It feels solid," he called back to Emma, who was lacing up her skates on the shore. "I think we're good to go."

Emma finished tying her skates and carefully stepped onto the ice. It felt sturdy under her feet, and she couldn't help but smile as she pushed off and glided smoothly across the surface. It had been years since she'd last skated, but the feeling came back to her quickly, the familiar thrill of skating across the ice making her heart soar.

Ben joined her, and soon they were skating together, laughing as they tried to outdo each other with spins and tricks. The air was filled with the sound of their laughter, echoing through the quiet woods. It was a moment of pure joy, the kind of simple pleasure that made life feel so full and rich.

After a while, they slowed down, catching their breath as they skated side by side, their hands clasped together. The cold air nipped at their cheeks, but their hearts were warm with the love they shared.

"This was a great idea," Emma said, her voice filled with happiness. "I'm so glad we decided to do this."

Ben smiled, giving her hand a squeeze. "Me too. I haven't had this much fun in a long time."

They continued to skate in silence for a few moments, simply enjoying the peacefulness of the morning and the beauty of the world around them. But as they made another pass across the pond, Emma noticed a faint crack running through the ice near the edge.

"Ben, look," she said, pointing to the crack. "Do you think the ice is safe?"

Ben frowned, skating over to examine it more closely. The crack was thin, but it stretched across a small section of the pond. "It's probably fine, but we should be careful. Let's stick to the center where it's thicker."

Emma nodded, feeling a slight unease settle in her stomach. They moved back toward the middle of the pond, continuing to skate but being more cautious now, listening for any signs of the ice weakening.

As they skated, Emma's mind began to wander, thinking about the conversation they'd had the night before about starting a family. She couldn't help but feel a sense of both excitement and anxiety about what the future might hold. They had come so far together, and she knew they were ready for whatever came next, but the unknown always carried a hint of fear.

Suddenly, there was a loud crack, followed by a sharp snapping sound. Emma's heart jumped into her throat as she looked down and saw a series of new cracks spidering out from beneath their skates.

"Ben!" she gasped, her voice tinged with panic.

Before they could react, the ice beneath them gave way with a loud splintering sound. In an instant, they were plunged into the icy water, the cold shock stealing the breath from Emma's lungs.

"Emma!" Ben shouted, his voice desperate as he reached for her.

The freezing water closed over Emma's head, and for a terrifying moment, she was completely disoriented, the cold numbing her senses. But then she felt Ben's hand grasp hers, pulling her back up to the surface.

They broke through the ice, gasping for air as they clung to the edge of the solid ice, their bodies trembling from the cold. Emma's heart raced, fear and adrenaline pumping through her veins as she struggled to catch her breath.

"Hold on," Ben said, his voice steady despite the panic in his eyes. "We need to stay calm and get out of here."

Emma nodded, fighting to keep her mind focused as she gripped the edge of the ice. With Ben's help, she managed to pull herself out of the water and onto the solid ice. Her entire body was shaking uncontrollably, the cold seeping into her bones.

Ben climbed out after her, his movements quick and deliberate. Once they were both on solid ground, he wrapped his arms around her, trying to warm her up. "We need to get back to the house, now," he said, his voice urgent. "You're freezing."

Emma nodded, unable to speak as her teeth chattered uncontrollably. They removed their skates as quickly as possible and made their way back to the house, moving as fast as they could through the snow. The cold air bit at their wet clothes, making the short walk feel like an eternity.

When they finally reached the house, Ben threw open the door and guided Emma inside. He quickly grabbed blankets and towels, wrapping Emma in them as she collapsed onto the couch, her entire body still trembling.

"Ben," she managed to say through chattering teeth, "I'm so cold."

"I know, I know," Ben said, his voice filled with concern as he rubbed her arms and legs, trying to get her warm. "Just hang in there, Emma. I'll get you warmed up."

He started a fire in the fireplace, the flames crackling to life and casting a warm glow over the room. As the heat began to fill the space, Emma felt a small measure of relief, but her body was still wracked with shivers.

Ben sat beside her, wrapping his arms around her and holding her close. "I'm so sorry, Emma. I shouldn't have taken us out on that ice. I should have been more careful."

Emma shook her head, tears stinging her eyes as she leaned into him. "It's not your fault, Ben. We didn't know. We're okay now, that's what matters."

They sat there for what felt like hours, slowly warming up as the fire crackled beside them. Emma's shivers eventually subsided, and she leaned back against Ben, feeling the warmth of his body seeping into her.

As the fear and adrenaline began to wear off, Emma felt a wave of exhaustion wash over her. But even as she closed her eyes, she couldn't shake the image of the ice breaking beneath them, the cold water pulling them under. It was a stark reminder of how quickly life could change, how fragile their plans and dreams could be.

Ben held her close, his hand gently stroking her hair. "I'm so glad you're okay, Emma. I don't know what I'd do if something happened to you."

Emma opened her eyes and looked up at him, her heart swelling with love and gratitude. "We're okay, Ben. We're together, and that's what matters."

They sat there in silence for a while longer, simply holding each other and finding comfort in the warmth of the fire and the strength of their love. The day had taken an unexpected turn, but as they sat together in their cozy living room, Emma knew that they could face anything as long as they were together.

Chapter 19: Reflections and Resolutions

The next morning, Emma awoke to the soft light of dawn filtering through the curtains. The events of the previous day still lingered in her mind, but she felt a sense of calm now that the initial shock had passed. She was warm, safe, and most importantly, she was with Ben.

She turned to find him already awake, his gaze fixed on her with a mix of concern and tenderness. "How are you feeling?" he asked, his voice gentle.

Emma stretched, feeling the warmth of the blankets wrapped around her. "A little sore, but I'm okay," she replied, managing a small smile. "Thank you for taking care of me last night."

Ben leaned in to kiss her forehead, his touch lingering as if he couldn't bear to let her go. "You scared me, Emma. I was so afraid something worse might have happened."

Emma placed a hand on his cheek, her heart swelling with affection. "But it didn't. We're both okay, and that's what matters. Let's just be more careful from now on."

Ben nodded, his expression softening. "Definitely. No more ice skating on ponds unless we're absolutely sure it's safe."

They shared a quiet moment, simply holding each other and finding comfort in their closeness. The near-miss on the ice had reminded them of how precious their time together was, and they weren't about to take it for granted.

After a while, they got up and made their way downstairs, the smell of freshly brewed coffee filling the air. Ben had already started breakfast, and the sight of the cozy kitchen, with its warm fire and the light snow falling outside, made Emma feel a deep sense of gratitude for the life they had built.

As they sat down to eat, Emma decided to bring up something that had been on her mind since the previous day. "Ben, I've been thinking about what happened yesterday, and it made me realize how quickly things can change. I don't want to live with any regrets, especially when it comes to us starting a family."

Ben looked at her, his eyes filled with understanding. "What are you saying, Emma?"

Emma took a deep breath, gathering her thoughts. "I think we should start trying to have a baby. I know we've been taking things one step at a time, but I don't want to wait any longer. I feel ready, and I want to take this next step with you."

Ben's expression softened, a smile spreading across his face. "I've been thinking the same thing. Yesterday was a wake-up call for me too, and I realized that I don't want to waste any more time. I want to start our family, Emma. I want to build a future with you."

Emma felt a surge of happiness and relief at his words. "I'm so glad we're on the same page. I've been feeling more and more that this is the right time for us."

Ben reached across the table, taking her hand in his. "Then let's do it, Emma. Let's start this new chapter together."

The decision made, they spent the rest of the morning talking about their plans, their hopes, and their dreams for the future. It was an exciting time, filled with the promise of new beginnings and the knowledge that they were ready to face whatever came their way together.

Over the next few weeks, they made small but meaningful changes to their lives, preparing for the possibility of a new addition to their family. They began to focus on their health, making sure they were both in the best possible shape. They also started to make changes to their home, slowly transforming the spare room into a cozy nursery.

As winter deepened, so did their bond. The quiet, snow-covered days gave them plenty of time to reflect on their journey and the love they shared. The idea of becoming parents brought a new level of excitement and anticipation to their lives, and it felt as though everything was falling into place.

One evening, as they sat together in the living room, Ben surprised Emma with a small gift. "I wanted to give you something," he said, handing her a beautifully wrapped box.

Emma looked at him curiously, her heart fluttering with anticipation. "What is it?"

"Open it and see," Ben said, his eyes twinkling with mischief.

Emma carefully unwrapped the box, revealing a delicate silver locket. She opened it to find two small compartments, each one designed to hold a tiny photograph. On one side, Ben had already placed a picture of the two of them, taken on the day of their wedding. The other side was empty, waiting to be filled.

"It's for our future," Ben explained softly. "One side for us, and the other for our family—our children, when they come. I wanted you to have something that represents the life we're building together."

Emma's eyes filled with tears as she looked up at him, overwhelmed by the thoughtfulness of the gift. "Ben, it's beautiful. I love it."

She leaned in to kiss him, her heart full to bursting with love and gratitude. "Thank you, Ben. This means so much to me."

They sat together in the warm glow of the fire, the locket resting gently against Emma's heart. It was a symbol of their journey, of the love they had found in each other, and of the life they were creating together.

As they looked toward the future, Emma knew that there would be challenges and uncertainties ahead. But she also knew that they would face them together, with the same strength and love that had brought them to this point.

Chapter 20: New Beginnings

The arrival of spring in Willow Creek brought a renewed sense of hope and energy to Emma and Ben's lives. The snow slowly melted away, revealing the vibrant colors of budding flowers and fresh green leaves. The town seemed to come alive again, with neighbors emerging from their winter hibernation, ready to embrace the warmer days ahead.

For Emma and Ben, the change in season mirrored the new beginnings they were preparing for. With the decision to start a family now firmly in place, they found themselves filled with excitement and a sense of purpose. Every day was a step closer to the future they had been dreaming of, and they were eager to embrace whatever lay ahead.

One morning, as Emma stood by the window, watching the first daffodils bloom in the garden, she felt a familiar flutter of excitement in her chest. She had always loved spring, with its promise of renewal and growth, but this year felt different. This year, she was not only looking forward to the beauty of the season but also to the possibility of creating new life.

As she turned away from the window, Ben walked into the room, his smile warm and bright. "Good morning," he said, wrapping his arms around her from behind. "You look like you're deep in thought."

Emma leaned back against him, a contented sigh escaping her lips. "I was just thinking about how beautiful everything is.

Spring always feels like a fresh start, and this year, it feels even more special."

Ben pressed a kiss to the top of her head, his arms tightening around her. "It does feel special. I can't help but feel like this is going to be our year, Emma. Everything we've dreamed about is within reach."

Emma smiled, turning in his arms to face him. "I feel the same way. And I can't wait to see what the future holds for us."

They spent the morning enjoying the sunshine, taking a leisurely walk through the town and greeting neighbors who were equally delighted by the arrival of spring. There was a sense of community and connection in the air, a reminder of why they had chosen to build their life in Willow Creek.

As they walked, they talked about their plans for the garden, which they had decided to expand this year. With the idea of starting a family in mind, they wanted to grow more of their own food, creating a space that was not only beautiful but also nourishing.

"We should plant more vegetables this year," Emma suggested, her mind already racing with ideas. "I'd love to have a little herb garden too, right outside the kitchen. It would be so nice to have fresh herbs for cooking."

Ben nodded, his enthusiasm matching hers. "I love that idea. We could also plant some fruit trees. Imagine having fresh apples and pears in the fall."

Emma's eyes lit up at the thought. "Yes! And maybe even a few berry bushes. We could make our own jams and pies."

As they planned their garden, it became clear that this project was about more than just growing food. It was about creating a home that was full of life and love, a place where they could nurture their dreams and build the future they wanted together.

The following weekend, they set to work on the garden, turning the soil and planting seeds with care and attention. It was hard work, but it was also deeply satisfying, and by the end of the day, they could already see the beginnings of what would soon be a lush, thriving space.

As they sat on the porch that evening, looking out over the freshly planted garden, Emma felt a sense of contentment settle over her. The world around them was filled with the promise of growth and renewal, and she knew that they were on the right path.

Ben reached over and took her hand, his fingers intertwining with hers. "We've come a long way, haven't we?"

Emma smiled, squeezing his hand. "We have. And it's been an incredible journey. I can't wait to see where it takes us next."

They sat in silence for a while, simply enjoying the peace of the evening and the sense of accomplishment that came from working together toward a common goal. The sky above them was painted in soft hues of pink and orange as the sun dipped below the horizon, and the first stars began to twinkle in the fading light.

As the days turned into weeks, the garden began to flourish, and so did Emma and Ben's anticipation for the future. They continued to prepare for the possibility of starting a family, taking small steps each day to ensure they were ready for whatever came their way.

One afternoon, as Emma was tending to the herb garden, she felt a sudden wave of dizziness wash over her. She paused, leaning on the garden hoe for support, and waited for the sensation to pass. When it did, she shrugged it off, assuming it was just from working too long in the sun.

But later that evening, when the dizziness returned, accompanied by a slight nausea, she couldn't ignore it any longer. A thought began to form in her mind, one that filled her with both excitement and nerves.

"Ben," she called from the kitchen, where she had been preparing dinner. "Can you come here for a moment?"

Ben appeared in the doorway, concern etched on his face. "What's wrong, Emma?"

Emma hesitated, searching for the right words. "I've been feeling a little off today—dizzy and nauseous. It might be nothing, but... I think it's possible that I could be pregnant."

Ben's eyes widened with surprise, and then his expression softened with hope. "Do you want to take a test, just to be sure?"

Emma nodded, her heart racing. "Yes, I think I should."

They made a quick trip to the pharmacy, the short drive filled with nervous anticipation. When they returned home, Emma went into the bathroom to take the test while Ben waited anxiously in the hallway.

After what felt like an eternity, Emma emerged, her hands trembling as she held the test in front of her. She met Ben's eyes, her own filled with a mixture of disbelief and joy.

"It's positive," she whispered, her voice thick with emotion. "Ben, we're going to have a baby."

Ben's face broke into a wide smile, and he pulled her into his arms, lifting her off the ground as he spun her around. "We're going to be parents!" he exclaimed, his voice filled with happiness.

Emma laughed through her tears, wrapping her arms around his neck. "I can't believe it. This is really happening."

They spent the rest of the evening in a state of bliss, talking about the future and what it would be like to welcome a new life into their world. The garden they had planted together now seemed like a symbol of the new beginning they were about to experience—a life filled with growth, love, and endless possibilities.

As they lay in bed that night, Emma felt a deep sense of peace and contentment wash over her. The future was bright, and she knew that whatever challenges came their way, they would face them together, with the same strength and love that had brought them to this point.

Chapter 21: Preparations and Promises

The news of Emma's pregnancy quickly spread through Willow Creek, filling the small town with excitement and joy. Friends and neighbors showered Emma and Ben with congratulations and well-wishes, and it wasn't long before the couple found themselves at the center of the community's attention. Everyone was eager to help in any way they could, from offering advice to volunteering their time and skills.

Emma and Ben embraced the support with open hearts, grateful for the love that surrounded them. The days quickly filled with preparations for the baby's arrival, and their home became a flurry of activity as they transformed the spare room into a nursery. They chose soft colors for the walls, a warm cream and pale yellow, and filled the space with furniture that spoke of comfort and safety.

As they worked together, Ben often caught Emma pausing to place a hand on her growing belly, a look of wonder in her eyes. It was a look that filled him with pride and a deep sense of responsibility. He had always known that starting a family would be a journey, but seeing Emma embrace motherhood with such grace and joy made him love her even more.

One afternoon, as they were assembling a crib, Ben looked over at Emma, who was carefully reading the instructions. "I can't believe we're really doing this," he said, his voice filled with awe. "In just a few months, we're going to be parents."

Emma looked up, a smile lighting up her face. "I know. It's hard to wrap my mind around it sometimes. But every time I feel the baby move, it makes it all feel so real."

Ben set down the pieces of the crib and walked over to her, placing a gentle hand on her belly. "I can't wait to meet our little one," he said softly, his eyes shining with love. "I promise you, Emma, I'm going to do everything I can to be the best father I can be."

Emma's heart swelled with emotion, and she reached up to cup his cheek. "You're already the best, Ben. This baby is so lucky to have you as a father."

They stood there for a moment, the room filled with the quiet anticipation of what was to come. The nursery was coming together beautifully, but it was the love they shared that truly made the space feel special.

As the weeks passed, the preparations continued. Emma and Ben attended childbirth classes, learned about caring for a newborn, and stocked up on everything they would need for the baby's arrival. They made sure to take time for themselves as well, cherishing the quiet moments they had together before their lives changed forever.

One evening, after a particularly busy day of preparations, they decided to take a walk through the town. The sun was setting, casting a warm golden light over the streets, and the air was filled with the scent of blooming flowers. As they strolled hand in hand, Emma couldn't help but feel a deep sense of contentment.

"Do you ever think about what life will be like once the baby is here?" Emma asked, her voice soft as they walked past the familiar shops and houses.

"All the time," Ben replied, glancing over at her with a smile. "I imagine sleepless nights, lots of diapers, and a house filled with baby toys. But more than that, I imagine all the little moments—reading bedtime stories, playing in the garden, watching our child grow and learn."

Emma smiled, her heart warm with the thought. "I can't wait for those moments. It's going to be a new adventure, one we get to experience together."

Ben nodded, squeezing her hand. "And whatever comes our way, we'll handle it. We've been through so much already, and we've come out stronger each time. This will be no different."

As they continued their walk, they passed by the town's park, where they had spent so many afternoons together. It was quiet now, with only a few families enjoying the evening, but Emma could already picture bringing their child here to play.

They sat down on a bench near the playground, watching the children laugh and chase each other across the grass. Emma felt a flutter in her belly and placed a hand over it, smiling at the familiar sensation.

"The baby's moving," she said, her voice filled with wonder.

Ben placed his hand over hers, his eyes lighting up. "I can feel it too. It's amazing."

They sat there in silence, simply enjoying the moment and the connection they felt with each other and their unborn child. The world around them seemed to fade away, leaving only the three of them in this perfect, peaceful moment.

As the sky darkened and the first stars began to appear, they made their way back home, the walk slow and filled with quiet conversation. They talked about names, about the kind of parents they wanted to be, and about the dreams they had for their child's future.

When they reached their front porch, Ben paused and turned to Emma, his expression serious. "Emma, I want you to know how much I love you. I've loved you since the day we met, and that love has only grown stronger with time. I can't wait to start this next chapter of our lives with you."

Emma felt tears prick at the corners of her eyes as she looked up at him. "I love you too, Ben. More than words can say. This baby... this family we're building together... it's everything I've ever wanted."

They embraced, holding each other close as the night settled around them. It was a moment filled with promise and hope, a moment that spoke of the future they were creating together.

As they went inside and prepared for bed, Emma felt a deep sense of peace. The days ahead would bring challenges, but she knew that with Ben by her side, they could face anything. Their love was strong, and it would carry them through whatever came their way.

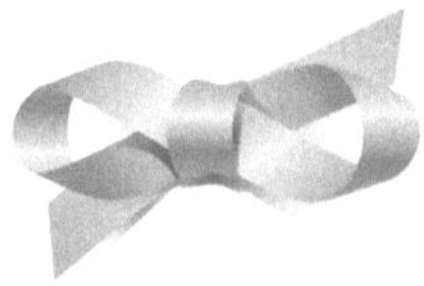

Chapter 22: The Unexpected

The following weeks passed in a blur of preparations, anticipation, and growing excitement. As Emma's due date approached, she and Ben found themselves both eager and anxious for the arrival of their baby. The nursery was ready, their bags were packed, and all that was left to do was wait.

One warm afternoon, as summer began to make its presence known in Willow Creek, Emma and Ben decided to take a final walk through the town before the baby arrived. The days were longer now, filled with the promise of new life and the warmth of the sun. As they walked, hand in hand, Emma couldn't help but marvel at how much had changed in the past year.

"It feels like just yesterday we were planning our wedding," Emma said, her voice filled with nostalgia. "And now here we are, about to become parents."

Ben smiled, squeezing her hand gently. "Time flies, doesn't it? But I wouldn't change a thing. Everything we've been through has led us to this moment, and I couldn't be happier."

As they continued their walk, they talked about the future and all the dreams they had for their growing family. It was a conversation filled with hope and excitement, the kind that made Emma's heart swell with love for the life they were creating together.

But as they neared the end of their walk, Emma suddenly felt a sharp pain in her abdomen. She stopped in her tracks, her hand instinctively going to her belly as she tried to steady herself.

"Emma? Are you okay?" Ben asked, concern etched across his face.

Emma took a deep breath, trying to assess what she was feeling. The pain was intense, but it quickly subsided, leaving her feeling slightly disoriented. "I... I think it was just a Braxton Hicks contraction," she said, trying to reassure both herself and Ben. "It's normal at this stage."

Ben didn't look entirely convinced, but he nodded. "Let's take it easy for the rest of the day, just in case. We don't want to push it."

Emma agreed, and they slowly made their way back home. She tried to relax, convincing herself that it was nothing more than the usual discomfort that came with the final weeks of pregnancy. But deep down, a part of her couldn't shake the feeling that something was different.

Later that evening, as they settled in for the night, the pain returned—this time stronger and more persistent. Emma winced, clutching her belly as the contraction gripped her.

"Ben," she said, her voice strained, "I think this might be it. The baby might be coming."

Ben's eyes widened with a mix of excitement and panic. "Okay, okay, let's get to the hospital."

They quickly grabbed their bags, their movements hurried but careful. The drive to the hospital felt like a blur, with Ben's focus entirely on getting Emma there safely while she tried to breathe through the contractions that were coming faster and harder.

When they arrived, the hospital staff quickly ushered them into a room, and before Emma knew it, she was hooked up to monitors, surrounded by nurses and doctors. The reality of what was happening began to sink in, and a wave of nervous anticipation washed over her.

"It's happening so fast," Emma whispered, her hand gripping Ben's as another contraction hit.

Ben leaned close, his voice calm and reassuring. "You're doing great, Emma. I'm right here with you. We're going to meet our baby soon."

The hours that followed were intense and exhausting, but Emma drew strength from Ben's presence and the thought of finally meeting their child. The contractions came one after another, each one bringing them closer to the moment they had been waiting for.

Finally, after what felt like an eternity, the doctor announced that it was time to push. Emma gathered every ounce of strength she had left, focusing on the sound of Ben's voice as he encouraged her with every breath.

"You're almost there, Emma," Ben said, his voice filled with emotion. "Just a little more."

With one final, powerful push, Emma felt a rush of relief as the room filled with the sound of a newborn's cry. Tears sprang to her eyes as the nurse gently placed the baby on her chest, and she looked down to see the tiny, perfect face of their child.

"It's a girl," the doctor announced with a smile. "Congratulations, Mom and Dad."

Emma's heart swelled with love as she gazed at the tiny life she had brought into the world. "She's beautiful," she whispered, tears streaming down her cheeks. "Ben, look at her."

Ben leaned in, his eyes wide with wonder as he looked at their daughter. "She's perfect, Emma. Absolutely perfect."

They sat there together, marveling at the miracle of their child, their hearts filled with a love that was beyond anything they had ever known. It was a moment of pure, unadulterated joy—the culmination of everything they had hoped and dreamed for.

As they held their daughter close, the world outside seemed to fade away. Nothing else mattered except the three of them, together at last, starting the next chapter of their lives as a family.

Chapter 23: Welcome Home

Bringing their daughter home was an experience filled with both excitement and a bit of nervousness for Emma and Ben. As they carefully carried the tiny bundle through the front door of their house, the reality of their new life as parents began to settle in.

The nursery, which had once felt like a project, now felt alive and full of purpose. The soft cream and pale yellow walls, the crib they had assembled together, and the little details they had lovingly chosen now served as the perfect backdrop for their baby girl.

Emma gently placed their daughter in the crib, watching as the baby blinked sleepily at the new surroundings. "Welcome home, sweetheart," Emma whispered, her heart swelling with love.

Ben stood beside her, wrapping an arm around her shoulders. "She's going to love it here," he said softly. "This is the perfect place to start our family."

Over the next few days, life settled into a new rhythm for Emma and Ben. The quiet, predictable routines they had known were replaced with the unpredictable but joyful chaos that comes with caring for a newborn. The nights were long, with feedings and diaper changes punctuating the hours, but neither of them minded. Every moment, even the sleepless ones, was filled with a sense of awe and gratitude.

Friends and neighbors from Willow Creek stopped by to drop off meals, gifts, and words of encouragement. The outpouring of support from the community reminded Emma and Ben of just how blessed they were to live in a place where they were surrounded by so much love and care.

One afternoon, Alyssa came by to visit, her arms laden with homemade meals and a few baby gifts. "I couldn't resist," she said with a grin as she set the bags down on the kitchen counter. "You know how I love to spoil my favorite little family."

Emma laughed, her heart warming at the sight of her friend. "You're amazing, Alyssa. We've barely had time to think about cooking, so these meals are a lifesaver."

Alyssa waved a hand dismissively. "It's the least I could do. How's the little one?"

"She's perfect," Ben said, his voice filled with pride as he gently rocked the baby in his arms. "We're still figuring everything out, but I think we're doing okay."

Alyssa smiled, watching them with a look of deep affection. "You two are doing more than okay. You're naturals. I can see how much love you already have for her."

Emma nodded, feeling a lump form in her throat. "It's overwhelming, in the best way. I never knew I could love someone so much."

They spent the afternoon chatting, sharing stories, and marveling at how much their lives had changed in such a short time. Alyssa held the baby for a while, her gentle rocking and soft cooing putting the little girl right to sleep. As Emma watched her friend with her daughter, she felt a deep sense of gratitude for the friendships that had sustained her through all the changes in her life.

After Alyssa left, Emma and Ben settled into the living room, the baby cradled in Emma's arms. The house was quiet, with only the soft sound of the baby's breathing filling the space. It was in these quiet moments that Emma felt the enormity of what they had created—the family they had dreamed of, now a reality.

Ben reached out and gently stroked the baby's cheek, his eyes filled with wonder. "I still can't believe she's ours," he said quietly. "It feels like a dream."

Emma smiled, leaning her head against his shoulder. "It's the best dream I've ever had. And it's real, Ben. We made this life together."

They sat in comfortable silence, simply enjoying the peace of the moment and the joy of being together as a family. The future was wide open, filled with endless possibilities, but for now, they were content to simply be in the moment, cherishing every second with their daughter.

As the days turned into weeks, Emma and Ben found their footing as parents. They learned to navigate the challenges of sleepless nights and fussy moments, finding comfort in each other and in the love they shared for their daughter. Each day brought new discoveries, new milestones, and a deeper connection to the life they had built together.

One evening, as they sat on the porch watching the sun set over Willow Creek, Ben turned to Emma with a thoughtful expression. "You know, I've been thinking a lot about how far we've come. We've built a beautiful life here, and now we have a family. It feels like everything we've ever wanted is finally falling into place."

Emma nodded, her heart full. "It does. And I'm so grateful for every step of the journey that brought us here."

Ben smiled, his eyes softening as he looked at her. "I couldn't have done any of this without you, Emma. You're my partner in everything, and I'm so thankful that we get to do this together."

Emma leaned in and kissed him, her voice filled with emotion. "I feel the same way, Ben. This life, this family... it's everything I've ever dreamed of."

As they sat together, holding their daughter close, the world around them seemed to pause. It was a moment of pure contentment, a reflection of all they had built together, and a promise of all the joy that was still to come.

Chapter 24: Embracing Parenthood

As summer fully settled over Willow Creek, Emma and Ben's new life as parents continued to blossom. The days were long and filled with the joyful chaos of caring for their daughter. Every morning brought a new adventure, from the first sleepy smiles to the tiny, curious hands reaching out to explore the world around her.

One warm afternoon, as Emma sat on the porch rocking their daughter to sleep, she marveled at how naturally this new chapter had unfolded. The tiny, delicate features of her daughter's face seemed like the most beautiful thing she had ever seen, and the weight of the little one in her arms felt like the most precious gift she had ever received.

Ben joined her on the porch, carrying two glasses of iced tea. He handed one to Emma and sat down beside her, watching as their daughter drifted off to sleep. "She's growing so fast," he said softly, a note of awe in his voice. "It feels like just yesterday we brought her home."

Emma nodded, taking a sip of her tea. "I know. It's hard to believe how quickly time is passing. Every day she changes, and I feel like I'm getting to know a new part of her."

Ben smiled, his gaze fixed on their daughter. "She's going to be incredible, Emma. I can already see so much of you in her—your strength, your kindness."

Emma felt a flush of warmth at his words. "And she has your determination and your sense of adventure. She's going to be amazing, Ben, because she has us to guide her."

They sat in companionable silence for a while, simply enjoying the peace of the afternoon. The garden they had planted earlier in the year was now in full bloom, the vibrant colors and fresh scents adding to the sense of tranquility that surrounded their home.

As the weeks passed, Emma and Ben settled into a routine, finding a balance between caring for their daughter and spending time together. They made a point of carving out moments just for themselves, whether it was sharing a quiet dinner after the baby was asleep or taking a walk through the town while a neighbor watched the little one.

One evening, as they sat together in the living room, Emma brought up something that had been on her mind. "Ben, have you thought about what's next for us? Now that we've settled into life with our daughter, do you think it's time to start thinking about the future?"

Ben looked thoughtful, setting down the book he had been reading. "I have been thinking about it, actually. We've come so far, and I feel like we're in such a good place right now. But I also know that there's more we want to do—more dreams we want to chase."

Emma nodded, her heart swelling with the possibilities. "I agree. I've been thinking about my work and how I want to balance being a mom and continuing to pursue my career. And I know you've been thinking about expanding your business too."

Ben smiled, reaching out to take her hand. "We can do both, Emma. We can build a life that fulfills us in every way, both as parents and as individuals. It's going to take some planning, but I know we can make it work."

Emma felt a sense of excitement building within her. "I love the idea of finding that balance. I want our daughter to see us following our passions, and I want her to know that she can do the same."

They spent the rest of the evening talking about their goals and dreams for the future, brainstorming ways to achieve them while maintaining the strong foundation they had built as a family. It was a conversation filled with hope and optimism, and by the end of it, Emma felt more energized and motivated than ever.

The following weekend, they decided to take a day trip to a nearby lake, a favorite spot they hadn't visited since before the baby was born. They packed a picnic, loaded up the car, and set off on the short drive, excited for a day of relaxation and fun.

When they arrived at the lake, they found a secluded spot by the water's edge, where the trees provided shade and the gentle lapping of the water created a soothing backdrop. Emma spread out a blanket while Ben set up a small umbrella to provide extra shade for their daughter.

As they settled in, Emma felt a deep sense of contentment. The lake was just as beautiful as she remembered, and the day promised to be one of those perfect summer days she had always cherished.

They spent the morning playing with their daughter, letting her feel the cool water on her tiny toes and watch the sunlight dance on the surface of the lake. The joy on her face was infectious, and Emma and Ben found themselves laughing more than they had in weeks.

After a leisurely lunch, Emma lay back on the blanket, the warm sun lulling her into a peaceful state of mind. Ben joined her, their daughter nestled between them, her tiny hand clutching Ben's finger as she drifted off to sleep.

"This is perfect," Emma said softly, her eyes half-closed as she soaked in the warmth of the day. "I couldn't ask for anything more."

Ben smiled, his voice filled with contentment. "Neither could I. This is what it's all about, Emma—these moments, this life we've created. I'm so grateful for everything we have."

They spent the rest of the day at the lake, savoring the peace and quiet, and enjoying the simple pleasure of being together. As the sun began to set, casting a golden glow over the water, they packed up their things and made their way back to the car, their hearts full from the day's adventures.

As they drove home, Emma felt a deep sense of gratitude for the life they had built together. The future was bright, and she knew that whatever challenges came their way, they would face them with the same strength, love, and determination that had carried them through so much already.

That night, as they tucked their daughter into her crib and settled into bed, Emma turned to Ben with a smile. "I can't wait to see what the future holds for us."

Ben wrapped his arm around her, pulling her close. "Whatever it is, we'll face it together. That's the best part."

Emma closed her eyes, feeling the warmth of his embrace and the steady beat of his heart. As she drifted off to sleep, she knew that this was just the beginning of a beautiful journey—one that she was grateful to share with the man she loved and the family they had created.

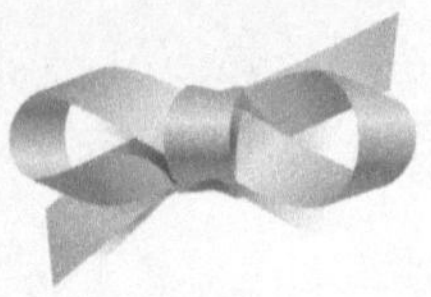

Chapter 25: Reflections and Resolutions

The summer continued to unfold in Willow Creek, bringing with it long, sunny days and warm, star-filled nights. Emma and Ben's daughter grew stronger and more curious with each passing week, and their home was filled with the laughter and joy that comes from watching a child discover the world.

One evening, as they sat together on the porch, Emma found herself reflecting on how far they had come. The last year had been a whirlwind of changes, from their wedding to the birth of their daughter, and now, as they settled into their new life as parents, she couldn't help but feel a deep sense of fulfillment.

Ben seemed to be in a similar frame of mind, his gaze fixed on the horizon as the sun dipped below the trees. "You know," he began, his voice thoughtful, "it's amazing to think about where we were a year ago. So much has changed, and yet, it feels like everything has fallen into place exactly as it was meant to."

Emma nodded, her heart swelling with affection for him. "I was just thinking the same thing. We've been through so much, and yet here we are, with everything we've ever wanted."

Ben turned to look at her, his eyes filled with love. "And it's only going to get better from here. We have so much to look forward to—watching our daughter grow up, continuing to build our life together."

Emma smiled, resting her head on his shoulder. "I can't wait. Every day feels like a new adventure, and I'm so grateful that we get to do this together."

They sat in silence for a while, simply enjoying the peace of the evening and the comfort of each other's presence. The sound of crickets chirping and the gentle rustling of the leaves in the breeze added to the sense of tranquility that surrounded them.

As the sky darkened and the stars began to twinkle overhead, Ben spoke again, his voice quiet but filled with conviction. "Emma, I've been thinking a lot about the future—about our dreams and goals. I want to make sure we're always moving forward, always striving to create the best life we can for ourselves and our daughter."

Emma lifted her head to look at him, her curiosity piqued. "What are you thinking?"

"I'm thinking that it's time to take some steps toward those dreams we talked about," Ben said, his gaze steady. "I want to expand my business, maybe take on some new projects that I've been putting off. And I want to support you in whatever you choose to do with your career. We've built a strong foundation, and now it's time to build on that."

Emma felt a surge of excitement at his words. "I love that idea, Ben. I've been thinking about my own goals too—about finding a way to balance being a mom with continuing to pursue my passions. It's important to me that our daughter sees us following our dreams, and I want to set that example for her."

Ben smiled, his hand finding hers. "We can do it, Emma. We've already accomplished so much together, and I have no doubt that we can achieve whatever we set our minds to."

They spent the rest of the evening talking about their plans for the future, brainstorming ideas and setting goals for the coming year. It was a conversation filled with hope and determination, and by the time they headed to bed, Emma felt a renewed sense of purpose.

The following weeks were a time of growth and change for both of them. Ben began to take on new challenges in his work, expanding his business and exploring new opportunities. Emma, too, found ways to balance her responsibilities as a mother with her professional aspirations, taking on projects that allowed her to pursue her passions while still being present for her family.

Their days were busy, but they made sure to prioritize their time together as a family. Whether it was a quiet morning walk with their daughter, a shared meal at the end of a long day, or simply sitting together on the porch as the sun set, they cherished the moments that reminded them of what truly mattered.

One evening, after a particularly successful day for both of them, Emma and Ben sat down to a celebratory dinner. Their daughter was asleep in her crib, and the house was quiet, save for the soft music playing in the background.

As they clinked their glasses together, Ben smiled at Emma, his eyes filled with pride. "I'm so proud of you, Emma. You've accomplished so much, and you've done it all while being an incredible mother. I couldn't ask for a better partner."

Emma blushed, feeling a wave of affection for him. "I couldn't have done any of it without you, Ben. You've been my rock through everything, and I'm so grateful for your support."

They spent the rest of the evening talking about the future, their dreams, and the life they were building together. It was a night filled with laughter, love, and the deep connection that had brought them through so much already.

As they cleared the dishes and prepared to head to bed, Emma felt a sense of contentment settle over her. The future was bright, and she knew that with Ben by her side, there was nothing they couldn't accomplish.

As they lay in bed that night, their hands intertwined, Emma whispered, "I love you, Ben. Thank you for making all of this possible."

Ben kissed her softly, his voice filled with emotion. "I love you too, Emma. This life we've created together—it's everything I've ever wanted."

As they drifted off to sleep, the stars shining brightly outside their window, Emma knew that this was just the beginning of a beautiful journey. The future was theirs to create, and she couldn't wait to see where it would take them.

Chapter 26: Celebrating Milestones

As autumn began to settle over Willow Creek, Emma and Ben found themselves reflecting on the many milestones they had reached in the past year. Their daughter was growing rapidly, each day bringing new surprises and small achievements that filled their hearts with pride. The crisp air and changing leaves outside mirrored the sense of change and growth happening within their home.

One particularly cool morning, as Emma was preparing breakfast, Ben walked into the kitchen with their daughter in his arms. The little girl was babbling happily, her bright eyes taking in everything around her.

"Good morning, my two favorite people," Emma said, smiling as she flipped a pancake. "Did you sleep well?"

Ben grinned, bouncing their daughter gently in his arms. "She slept like a champ, and so did I. I think we're finally getting the hang of this parenting thing."

Emma laughed, setting the pancake on a plate and turning to face them. "It only took us a year, right? But seriously, I feel like we're in such a good place now. We've come so far."

As they sat down to breakfast, they talked about the upcoming weekend, when they would be celebrating their daughter's first birthday. The event had been a topic of conversation for weeks, and Emma had been meticulously planning every detail.

"I can't believe she's already turning one," Emma said, her voice tinged with nostalgia. "This year has gone by so fast. It feels like just yesterday we were bringing her home from the hospital."

Ben reached across the table to take her hand, his expression filled with warmth. "She's growing up so quickly, and she's so amazing, Emma. I can't wait to see what the next year brings."

They spent the day preparing for the party, which was set to take place in their backyard. The garden, still vibrant with the colors of late summer, provided the perfect backdrop for the celebration. Emma and Ben hung decorations, set up tables, and made sure everything was just right for the special day.

When the weekend arrived, their home was filled with friends, family, and neighbors who had all come to celebrate. The backyard buzzed with laughter and conversation, and the smell of barbecue wafted through the air. The party was a joyful occasion, filled with love and happiness.

Emma watched as their daughter, now a confident toddler, toddled around the yard with the help of Ben's guiding hands. The little girl's face was a picture of pure delight as she explored her surroundings, her laughter ringing out like music.

As the day went on, Emma found herself surrounded by the people who had supported her and Ben through the many changes in their lives. Alyssa was there, of course, along with several of their closest friends from Willow Creek. It was a day of connection and reflection, a celebration not just of their daughter's first year but of the life they had built together.

When it came time for the cake, everyone gathered around, watching as Emma and Ben helped their daughter blow out the single candle. The little girl's face lit up with excitement as everyone clapped and cheered, and Emma couldn't help but feel a wave of emotion wash over her.

Later that evening, after the last of their guests had left and the house was quiet again, Emma and Ben sat together in the living room, their daughter asleep in her crib upstairs. They were both tired but happy, their hearts full from the day's events.

"That was a perfect day," Ben said, leaning back against the couch with a contented sigh. "I think our little girl had the time of her life."

Emma smiled, resting her head on his shoulder. "She did. And so did I. I couldn't have asked for a better way to celebrate her first year."

Ben wrapped his arm around her, pulling her close. "I'm so proud of us, Emma. We've made it through an entire year of parenting, and I think we're doing pretty well."

Emma nodded, feeling a deep sense of accomplishment. "We are. And it's only going to get better from here. I'm excited to see what the future holds for us."

They sat in silence for a while, simply enjoying the peace and quiet of the evening. The house, now filled with memories of the day's celebration, felt warm and welcoming, a true reflection of the life they had built together.

As they headed to bed that night, Emma couldn't help but feel a sense of closure. The past year had been filled with so many changes, so much growth, and as they moved forward into the next chapter of their lives, she knew that they were ready for whatever came next.

Chapter 27: A Year of Gratitude

As the autumn leaves turned golden and the days grew shorter, Emma and Ben found themselves in a reflective mood. The celebration of their daughter's first birthday had been a significant milestone, and now, as they settled back into their daily routines, they couldn't help but look back on the year that had passed.

One crisp evening, after putting their daughter to bed, Emma suggested a walk through Willow Creek. The cool air and the peacefulness of the town at twilight had always been soothing to her, and she knew it would be the perfect way to unwind after a busy day.

"Let's take a walk," Emma said, pulling on her jacket. "It's such a beautiful night, and I think we could both use a little fresh air."

Ben agreed, and soon they were strolling hand in hand down the quiet streets, the golden glow of the streetlights casting a warm hue over the town. The crunch of leaves underfoot and the distant sound of crickets created a serene atmosphere that made Emma feel deeply connected to the world around her.

As they walked, they talked about the year that had passed, about the challenges they had faced and the joys they had experienced. It was a conversation filled with gratitude, as they both realized how much they had grown, both individually and as a couple.

"It's amazing to think about everything we've been through," Emma said, her voice soft. "This time last year, we were just starting to figure out what it meant to be parents, and now look at us. We've made it through a whole year, and our daughter is thriving."

Ben smiled, squeezing her hand. "We've come a long way, haven't we? And I'm so proud of us, Emma. We've created something beautiful together—a life, a family, a home."

Emma felt a lump form in her throat as she looked up at him, her heart swelling with emotion. "I'm proud of us too, Ben. And I'm so grateful for everything we have. This past year has been the best of my life, and I know it's just the beginning."

As they continued their walk, they found themselves at the edge of the park, where the town's harvest festival was just wrapping up for the evening. The sight of the colorful tents and the sound of laughter brought back memories of their first days in Willow Creek, when everything had felt new and uncertain.

"Do you remember our first harvest festival here?" Emma asked, smiling at the memory. "We had no idea what the future held, but we were so excited to start this new chapter."

Ben nodded, a nostalgic smile on his face. "I remember. And look at us now—so much has changed, but that excitement is still there. We've built a life here, and it's more than I ever could have imagined."

They watched as the last of the festivalgoers packed up their belongings and headed home, leaving the park peaceful and quiet once more. The sight of the empty tents and the lingering scent of caramel apples and cinnamon made Emma feel a deep sense of contentment.

As they turned to head back home, Emma paused for a moment, taking in the beauty of the night and the overwhelming gratitude she felt. "I never want to take any of this for granted," she said softly. "This life we've created—it's everything I've ever wanted."

Ben wrapped his arm around her, pulling her close. "I feel the same way, Emma. We've been through so much, and I'm so thankful for every moment we've shared. I can't wait to see what the future holds for us."

When they arrived home, the house was warm and inviting, the glow of the porch light welcoming them back. As they stepped inside, Emma felt a sense of peace settle over her. This was her home, her family, her life—and she wouldn't trade it for anything.

That night, as they lay in bed, Emma couldn't help but reflect on how far they had come. The past year had been filled with so many milestones, so much growth, and as they moved forward, she knew that they were ready for whatever came next.

Chapter 28: A Season of Change

As the chill of autumn deepened and the leaves turned to shades of gold and crimson, Emma and Ben found themselves preparing for the upcoming holidays. Willow Creek was already beginning to embrace the season, with decorations going up in the town square and the scent of pumpkin spice and pine needles lingering in the air. For Emma, the holidays had always been a time of joy and reflection, but this year felt particularly special.

One morning, as Emma was dressing their daughter in a cozy sweater and tiny boots, Ben walked into the room, holding a cup of coffee and a letter in his hand. His expression was one of curiosity and excitement.

"Emma, look what came in the mail today," he said, handing her the letter.

Emma took the letter, recognizing the handwriting on the envelope immediately. "It's from my parents," she said, her heart skipping a beat. "I wonder what they're up to."

She carefully opened the letter and began to read. As her eyes scanned the familiar handwriting, a smile spread across her face. "They want to come visit for Thanksgiving," she said, looking up at Ben. "They're hoping to spend the holiday with us and meet their granddaughter for the first time."

Ben's face lit up with excitement. "That's wonderful, Emma! It'll be great to have them here and to celebrate the holiday together as a family."

Emma felt a warm sense of anticipation building inside her. Thanksgiving had always been a cherished tradition in her family, and the thought of sharing it with her parents, Ben, and their daughter filled her with joy. "I can't wait to see them," she said, her voice tinged with emotion. "It's been too long since we've all been together."

The days leading up to Thanksgiving were filled with preparations. Emma and Ben worked together to make sure everything was perfect, from planning the menu to decorating the house with autumnal touches. Their daughter, now more curious than ever, toddled around the house, her laughter filling the rooms as she explored every corner.

When Emma's parents arrived, the reunion was everything she had hoped for. Her mother immediately scooped up her granddaughter, showering her with kisses and exclamations of delight, while her father beamed with pride as he watched his family together in one place.

The holiday itself was a beautiful celebration of love, gratitude, and togetherness. The house was filled with the delicious aromas of roasted turkey, stuffing, and freshly baked pies. Laughter echoed through the rooms as stories were shared, and the warmth of the fire in the living room created a cozy atmosphere that made everyone feel at home.

As they all sat down to dinner, Emma couldn't help but feel a deep sense of contentment. The table was surrounded by the people she loved most, and the room was filled with the kind of joy that only comes from being with family. It was a moment of pure happiness, one that she knew she would cherish for the rest of her life.

After dinner, as everyone gathered in the living room to relax and enjoy dessert, Emma's mother turned to her with a thoughtful expression. "Emma, I just want to say how proud I am of you," she said, her voice filled with emotion. "You've built a beautiful life here, and it's clear how much love and happiness you've brought to this family."

Emma felt tears prick at the corners of her eyes as she reached out to take her mother's hand. "Thank you, Mom. That means so much to me. I'm so grateful for everything we have, and I'm so happy that you're here to share it with us."

As the evening drew to a close, Emma and Ben tucked their daughter into bed, her tiny body nestled under a warm quilt. The house was quiet now, the only sound the soft crackling of the fire in the hearth. Emma and Ben stood together by the crib, watching their daughter sleep, her face peaceful and content.

"She's so perfect," Ben whispered, his voice filled with awe. "Every day, I'm amazed by her—and by you, Emma. You've given me everything I've ever wanted."

Emma turned to him, her heart swelling with love. "And you've given me the same, Ben. This life we've created—it's more than I ever dreamed of."

They held each other close, their hearts full of gratitude for the life they had built together. The season of change had brought them so much joy, and as they looked toward the future, they knew that whatever challenges or blessings lay ahead, they would face them together.

Chapter 29: The Magic of Christmas

As the last of the autumn leaves fell and the first snow of the season blanketed Willow Creek, Emma and Ben turned their attention to preparing for their daughter's first Christmas. The holiday season had always held a special place in Emma's heart, but this year, with a child of their own, it felt even more magical.

The town came alive with holiday cheer, the streets lined with twinkling lights and festive decorations. The scent of pine and cinnamon wafted through the air, and the sound of carolers filled the evenings with warmth and joy. Willow Creek's annual Christmas tree lighting in the town square was a tradition that Emma and Ben eagerly anticipated, and this year, they were excited to share it with their daughter.

One afternoon, as they were decorating their home for the holidays, Ben brought in a freshly cut Christmas tree. Emma had always insisted on having a real tree, loving the scent and the tradition of picking one out together. Their daughter watched with wide eyes as Ben set the tree up in the living room, her tiny hands reaching out to touch the soft needles.

"This is going to be the best Christmas yet," Emma said, smiling as she handed Ben a string of lights. "I can't wait to see her face on Christmas morning."

Ben nodded, a grin spreading across his face. "She's going to love it. And I can't wait to start all our Christmas traditions with her—decorating the tree, baking cookies, reading 'Twas the Night Before Christmas.'"

They spent the rest of the day decorating the tree, carefully placing ornaments they had collected over the years, each one holding a special memory. The final touch was the star on top, which Ben lifted their daughter up to place with her tiny hands, the moment filled with laughter and love.

As Christmas Day approached, the excitement in their home grew. Emma baked cookies and wrapped presents, filling the house with the smells and sights of the season. Ben helped their daughter write a letter to Santa, her scribbles more enthusiastic than legible, but the effort was met with proud smiles and encouragement.

The night before Christmas, after putting their daughter to bed, Emma and Ben sat together by the fire, enjoying the quiet moment of peace before the festivities of the next day. The tree lights twinkled softly, casting a warm glow over the room, and outside, the snow fell gently, covering the world in a blanket of white.

"This is perfect," Emma said, leaning her head on Ben's shoulder. "I feel like everything we've been working toward, everything we've dreamed of, is right here."

Ben kissed the top of her head, his voice soft. "It is. This is what it's all about, Emma. We've built something beautiful together, and now we get to share it with our daughter. I couldn't ask for anything more."

They sat in silence for a while, simply enjoying the moment and the deep connection they shared. The anticipation of Christmas morning filled the air, and as they finally headed to bed, Emma felt a sense of contentment she had never known before.

Christmas morning arrived with the sound of their daughter's excited giggles as she discovered the gifts under the tree. The sight of her wide-eyed wonder as she tore into the wrapping paper, revealing the surprises within, filled Emma's heart with joy. The day was spent in the company of family, with a delicious meal, laughter, and the warmth of love that made the holiday truly special.

As the day drew to a close, and the last of the guests had left, Emma and Ben sat together by the fire, their daughter asleep in Ben's arms. The room was quiet, the soft glow of the tree lights reflecting in their eyes as they looked at each other, knowing that this moment was one they would treasure forever.

"This has been the best Christmas," Emma whispered, her voice filled with emotion. "I'm so grateful for everything we have, for this life we've created."

Ben nodded, his eyes shining with love. "I am too, Emma. This is everything I've ever wanted—and more."

They sat there for a long time, simply holding each other and soaking in the magic of the season. The snow continued to fall outside, the world peaceful and still, and in that moment, Emma knew that they had everything they needed.

Chapter 30: New Year's Reflections

As the final days of December unfolded, Willow Creek settled into the quiet calm that comes between Christmas and the New Year. The town, still adorned with festive decorations, took on a serene atmosphere as the year drew to a close. For Emma and Ben, it was a time of reflection, gratitude, and the anticipation of what was to come.

On New Year's Eve, after putting their daughter to bed, Emma and Ben decided to have a quiet evening at home. They had always enjoyed celebrating the start of a new year together, but this year, they wanted to keep things simple, focusing on the moments that mattered most.

They prepared a special dinner, filled with their favorite foods, and set the table with candles and the good china. As they sat down to eat, the soft glow of the candles casting a warm light over the room, Emma couldn't help but feel a deep sense of peace.

"This has been an incredible year," Emma said, her voice filled with emotion. "So much has happened, and I feel like we've grown so much as a family."

Ben nodded, his eyes reflecting the same sentiment. "It has been incredible, hasn't it? We've faced challenges, but we've also had so many beautiful moments. I'm so grateful for everything we've built together."

After dinner, they moved to the living room, where the fire crackled softly in the hearth. They sat together on the couch, their hands intertwined, as they talked about the year that had passed and their hopes for the year ahead.

"I feel like we've found our rhythm," Ben said, his voice thoughtful. "We've learned so much about being parents, about being partners, and I think we're in a really good place. I'm excited to see where the next year takes us."

Emma smiled, leaning her head on his shoulder. "Me too. There's so much to look forward to, and I'm so glad we get to do it together."

As midnight approached, they turned on the television to watch the countdown to the New Year. The excitement of the moment was palpable, and as the clock ticked down the final seconds, they held each other close, ready to welcome whatever the future held.

"Three, two, one... Happy New Year!" they both exclaimed, sharing a kiss as the fireworks lit up the screen.

The sound of the celebrations outside filled the air, and for a moment, they simply held each other, the promise of a new beginning filling their hearts.

As the excitement of the moment faded, they sat back down on the couch, their hands still intertwined. The fire crackled softly, and outside, the snow continued to fall, blanketing the world in a layer of fresh, untouched beauty.

"Do you have any resolutions for the new year?" Ben asked, his voice soft as he looked at Emma.

Emma thought for a moment, then smiled. "I think my resolution is to keep appreciating the little moments. This past year has taught me how important it is to savor the time we have together, to not take anything for granted. I want to carry that with me into the new year."

Ben nodded, his expression thoughtful. "I like that. I think mine is to keep growing—both as a father and as a partner. I want to keep learning, keep improving, and keep building this life we've started together."

They sat in comfortable silence for a while, simply enjoying the peace of the moment and the warmth of the fire. The new year stretched out before them, filled with endless possibilities, and as they looked toward the future, they felt ready for whatever came their way.

Eventually, they decided to head to bed, the excitement of the evening giving way to the quiet calm of the night. As they climbed the stairs, Emma paused at the door to their daughter's room, peeking in to check on her. The little girl was sound asleep, her tiny body curled up under a soft blanket, her face peaceful and content.

Emma felt a wave of love and gratitude wash over her as she watched her daughter sleep. This was her family, her life, and it was more than she had ever dreamed of. She knew that the year ahead would bring its own set of challenges and joys, but she also knew that they would face them together, with the same strength and love that had carried them through so much already.

As they climbed into bed, Ben wrapped his arms around her, pulling her close. "Happy New Year, Emma," he whispered, his voice filled with affection.

"Happy New Year, Ben," she replied, feeling the warmth of his embrace and the steady beat of his heart against hers. "I can't wait to see what the future holds for us."

As they drifted off to sleep, the snow continued to fall outside, the world peaceful and still. The promise of a new beginning filled the air, and in that moment, Emma knew that they were exactly where they were meant to be.

Don't miss out!

Visit the website below and you can sign up to receive emails whenever Gracelynne MacAllister publishes a new book. There's no charge and no obligation.

https://books2read.com/r/B-A-CCFLC-TMYKF

Connecting independent readers to independent writers.